You Mean Something

Woods Lake #2 – Jesse & Lexie

JLYNN AUTUMN

Important Notice

"This book is a work of fiction. The names, characters, places and incidents are products of the writer's imagination or have been used fictitiously and are not to be construed as real. Any resemblance to persons, living or dead, actual events, locales, or organization is entirely coincidental."

DEDICATION

To Robert, who has always been my biggest fan and supporter. The only one who has ever meant something. The one who loved me so much I learned to forget the hurt and pain from my past and accept love that I never knew I deserved.

You Mean Something

Chapter 1

Jesse

Tony called out to me as I crossed the bar area. "Jesse, you're drinking on us. What do you want?" It was busy in here tonight. The bar was three deep across with people waiting to order and every table was taken. The dance floor was packed. The line outside went to the end of the building.

"Whatever lager you have on tap. Thanks, Tony." I walked up to the end of the bar that technically wasn't a customer space but was the spot for employees to go back and forth. "Since when is it this busy in the middle of the week?"

"It's summer. Everyone is back home, and we are the only place in town open past eight. We're slammed seven days a week right now. Thanks for covering the door until Dad could get here. I appreciate it. I can't believe our door guy called out again tonight. It's going to be his last night on the payroll."

"Well, I'm done at the garage by six almost every night, so text if you need the door or the bar covered. I don't mind helping out a couple of nights a week. There's no point bringing on more staff if it's just for the summer."

"Thanks. I appreciate it." He handed me my beer.

"That's what family's for cousin. Is the bar covered the rest of the night or are you going to get slammed working by yourself? You're already three deep and the line outside goes to the end of the building. I'm off tomorrow, so I don't mind working if you need me to, but if I'm pouring, this needs to be my one and done."

Tony glanced across the room. I could tell he wanted to ask me to help. He turned back to me. "I'll let you know by the time you finish that one. I'm handling it so far, but it was supposed to be Dad and me behind the bar tonight."

"I'll plan on this one and then get ready to help" I took a sip of my beer as I grabbed a bowl of pretzels.

"You're my favorite cousin."

"Just until you need your piece of shit truck fixed and you tell Marco that same line so you can use his home shop and not have to pay us at the garage."

"Basically."

I glanced at the table in the back corner that was covered in balloons and gifts. A group of six or seven girls surrounded the table. I didn't recognize any of them, but I couldn't see who was sitting behind the pile of gift bags. The girls I could see were definitely from the city. They were dressed in tight short dresses and heels. Way too fancy for Rocky's. This was a low key bar. Not quite a dive, but casual and low key was more the overall style here. "What's up with the group in the corner? Birthday party or something?"

"Bachelorette celebration." Tony filled two pitchers and stacked eight glasses on the bar for the large group of guys who had taken over the four middle tables watching the baseball game.

"Whose?" I glanced over at the table again trying to figure out if I recognized any of them.

"Brie Gomes."

"Third time's a charm?" I take another sip of my beer and glance at the label on the tap to read which craft brewery this one was from.

A soft voice next to me says, "Or three strikes you're out."

I look over and see Lexie. Damn, she's more gorgeous than when I saw her in here a few months ago. She's just under shoulder height to me. Her eyes sparkle and are a shade of blue that sometimes appear gray. Her hair is that amazing brown that appears auburn under certain lights. "Hey, Lexie. Sorry, I wasn't being an ass about your sister. I'm going to be covering the bar in a few, just seeing what's going on tonight."

"Didn't think you were being an ass, Jesse. I already told her it's three strikes you're out. I'm not doing the bridesmaid thing again and I'm not throwing her more parties, but I am looking forward to her being out of my apartment."

I set my beer down and leaned on the bar next to her. I turned to her as I spoke. "When's the wedding?"

"Next week, Thursday night. Thank God. I rented a studio when she got married the first time and got rid of our two-bedroom apartment. She still thinks my place is 'our' place and she crashes whenever she's single. I'm so ready for her to be out. I love her because she's my sister, but I don't like her, you know what I mean?"

"I do. I think we all have family members like that. They're people we love because they're family, but we wouldn't choose them as friends."

"Exactly."

"So why are you hanging out at the bar instead of at the party?"

"I know one person and I share DNA with her and since she's been living with me for the past four months, I need a break."

"Makes sense. Can I buy you a drink?"

"I'm driving. I'll take a club soda with lime though. Thanks, Jesse."

"There's a table for two available in the corner that opened, go grab it. I'll bring you your drink and join you while I finish this before Tony needs me behind the bar. We can catch up and I'll be your excuse to be away from the party."

"Sounds like fun." She turned and walked to the table in the corner.

I went behind the bar and poured her drink, grabbed more pretzels, topped off my beer, and grabbed a bottled water. Tony reached his arm out behind him as he slid a beer to the customer he was helping. I took the hint and stopped. He turned to me and stared at me eye-to-eye. We were both six foot three and most people thought we were siblings, not cousins because we had the same dark brown almost black eyes, dark brown hair, and had grown up in the same house most of the time. I was four years older than him, but when it came to Lexie and Brie, he always played the big brother card. He had been best friends with Brie since Kindergarten. "Jesse, a piece of advice, be careful. Lexie's a sweet girl and her ex pulled a number on her."

I shook my head before I spoke. "Tony, we both know I'm not a relationship guy, and she's a relationship girl. I'm giving her an out that she needs. She's always been a sweetheart. I have no plans of going there."

"I had to say it."

"I know. I get why. Plus, isn't she barely legal to be in here?"

"She's 22."

"I'm 28. If I was looking for a relationship, which I'm not, I'm not looking for a child."

I took our drinks and pretzels to the table. I set everything down and hopped up on the barstool. "Lexie, catch me up on your life. It's been ages since we've had a conversation other than 'hi' and 'have fun' when I'm working the door."

"I'm teaching art classes at the community center this summer and they've been really popular. The director asked me to teach again in the fall. I like not having to drive to the city to get work as an art teacher. I still have to do it, but not every day now. I teach two days a week in town and three in the city. Teaching art classes doesn't completely pay the bills so I do graphic design independently which gives me the flexibility to work from home or anywhere else and I can set my hours around when I am teaching. I recently finished a job for Rocky. I redesigned the table tent cards, letterhead, and business cards for the bar. He wants me to do the new letterhead and business cards for the rental property next. None of it needs to be done, but he likes giving me work when he can."

"Fantastic. Are you still painting and doing your artwork?" I took a sip from my beer and grabbed a couple of pretzels.

"I was until about four months ago when I had to make room in the studio for my sister."

"You'll start again next week then?" I smiled at her as we both reached for pretzels. I moved my hand back to let her go first.

She nodded her head and spoke softly. "I'm going to be showing at the end of summer festival. We're doing a show of student artwork too. Everything will be for sale and we are hoping to raise enough money to fund a few additional classes."

"That's amazing Lexie. It's nice the town is starting to have more stuff for kids. There was nothing to do in this town growing up except get in trouble."

"It's why I decided to move back to town after art school. I wanted to bring an opportunity to town that I didn't have growing up. I was always the weird art girl that never fit in because I'm super shy, would rather being reading or painting, and there were exactly zero art classes offered all through school."

I laughed a little. "Since when are you shy?"

"Since forever."

"But you're talking to me and telling me everything."

"I've known you my entire life, Jesse. It's different. Now it's your turn. Tell me everything." She grabbed a couple of pretzels and took a sip of her drink.

"Not much to tell. I cover the door or bar here when they're short because they're family. I work for Marco at the garage, but we recently worked out an arrangement for part of my paycheck to go toward buying into the business. When the contract is done, I'll own twenty percent of the garage. I bought that two-bedroom, one-bath house on Maple that's been for sale for almost two years. I've been fixing it up on my days off."

"The house that when we were growing up the super sweet older couple lived in with the big orange tree in the front yard?" I nodded as I took a sip of my beer. I caught Brie staring at us from across the room, from the corner of my eye, but didn't break eye contact with Lexie as she spoke. Her blue-gray eyes captivated me, and I couldn't not look at her. "I always loved that house. I used to walk the long way home from school so I could walk past it especially when the orange blossoms bloomed. I loved the smell. I always thought the front porch would be perfect to sketch and paint on."

"That's the one. He passed away about six years ago and she passed a little over a year after that. They didn't have kids. When a family member was finally found, they way overpriced it for this area. I contacted them and told them some stories about Marco and me helping take care of the yard and climbing the tree to pick oranges when we were kids. I low balled my offer thinking they'd counter, but they accepted."

"Amazing Jesse. Please don't do something drastic and get rid of the porch."

I set my elbows on the table and leaned forward a bit. "No, never. I love that porch. So that catches you up on me. My life is work, fixing up the house, helping here every once in a while, and Sunday night dinners at Marco's. My aunt would have my ass if I didn't show."

"Sounds like you stay busy." She took a sip from her drink.

"You too, right? Teaching art classes and doing graphic design must keep you busy."

"Yeah, but you have people in your life. I teach kids and then the rest of my life is independent, which I love for the freedom it gives me to work when I went and be set to someone else's schedule, but this is the most adult conversation I've had in months other than my sister."

"You need to come hang here. It's a small town. You'll see people you know." We both reached for pretzels again and laughed as I pulled my hand back so she could grab first. I took a sip from my beer and then grabbed a few pretzels.

"Not my scene. I do it when I get dragged out, but I'm more a small get together person. I'm not a fan of crowds and big groups where I don't know a lot of people. I'm a total nerd Jesse. Backyard BBQs, pool hangouts, poker, or video game are more my speed."

"If you tell me you know how to cook, you might change my opinion on relationships. I love barbecues, pool hangouts, poker, and I'm a video game nerd." She squinted her eyes together a bit. "What's that face?"

She smiled. "I've been warned and heard stories about your opinion on relationships."

I shrugged my shoulders. "It's not something I hide. I don't do relationships. I have no interest in getting married or having kids. I'm honest about that from the start. I'm a fun guy for a weekend, or a week, or a few weeks at most. Then girls move on because they realize I was serious when I said I don't do relationships."

"At least you're honest about it and don't hide it." There was a hurt in her eyes when she said it. For the first time since I sat down, she broke eye contact. Her eyes dropped to look at her hands and she bit her lower lip.

"I'm a firm believer in what you see is what you get and with me, you get someone to hang out and do things with and have the freedom to walk away anytime because I'm not looking for a commitment." I touched her hand. Her eyes locked on mine. I lowered my voice a bit. "I don't know what he did Lexie, but if he let you walk away or pushed you away, it's his loss."

She smiled at me. "Thanks, Jesse. I should let you get to the bar. Thanks for the drink and the chat." She got up and started to walk away. I don't know what came over me, but I reached out my arm, took her hand, and pulled her back to me. "Lexie, what are you doing tomorrow? Do you want to come to see what I've done to the house? The orange tree just blossomed."

"I teach morning studio classes in town. I'm done at 11."

"I'm off, so come by after. I'll be there."

"Okay."

She headed to the corner where the bachelorette party was set up and I headed to the bar. I threw our glasses in the dishwasher and washed my hands at the sink before starting to help Tony get the line down. I kept my eye on the corner throughout the night. When the line got down, Tony caught me looking at Lexie across the room.

"How was your chat?"

I looked at him. "It was fun to catch up. I think it's probably the most the two of us have talked one on one our entire lives. She's a sweet girl. You're right, definitely hurt by whatever jackass she was dating. Shame, because she's sweet and would be good for someone who was actually looking for something."

Tony shook his head slowly and smiled. "Are you sure you're not looking for something and that maybe you just haven't found it because you haven't found the one who means anything?"

"Nope." I shook my head. "I'm fun for a weekend or week at most, but I've never done the relationship thing and don't plan on it."

"Right. Keep telling yourself that. You find the right one and you know. It hits you and everything changes." He wiped down the bar area where three people had just left.

"Says the guy who let the right one walk away how many times?" I looked at him and waited for a response.

"Lucy and I are trying to figure things out. There are a few things that I can't deal with anymore and I needed a break."

"The ranting and yelling about a certain friendship that she doesn't trust and never has finally enough to send you over the edge?"

He glanced over at me and nodded. "Yep. Hopefully, we figure it out because she's the one. I know she is, but I can't deal with the jealousy. I can't deal with the yelling and the trust issues. It's only ever been Lucy since I was twenty. She was it for me the night I met her. I hope we can figure things out, but it's not working right now."

I wiped down the bar space that had cleared and started unloading the glasses that had finished in the dishwasher. "You two will figure it out. Keep trying. She's worth it."

"She's definitely worth it Jesse. Everything's better when she's around. You'll find it someday and know what I mean."

"Not a marriage and kid guy. You know that and you know why." I leaned against the back counter of the bar as we talked.

Tony came and stood next to me. "I get it. You bounced between us and Marco's house growing up and your parents were gone most of the time. It has to be hard, but not wanting marriage and kids doesn't mean you don't want something that means something, Jesse. Don't write off all relationships. Not all relationships have to lead to kids and a picket fence."

"I already have a picket fence, remember?" I laughed and walked to the other side of the bar to help the group that had walked up.

Chapter 2

Lexie

"**W**hat was that?" Brie asked as soon as I got back to the tables.

"What was what?" I knew she meant Jesse but was playing it off like it was no big deal.

"Don't play that game. We all saw you with Jesse. I warned you when you moved back to town after art school in the city that he was trouble. He's fun for a weekend guy, not a relationship guy."

"Perfect because the last thing on Earth I need or want is a relationship. We were catching up. It's been ages since we've actually talked. He had some time to kill before he needed to be behind the bar, and I didn't think you'd mind. It's not like I know any of these friends."

"Be careful." She wrapped her arm over my shoulder like she does when she's been drinking. Tipsy Brie clue number one. Clue two, the high-pitched giggle, would start soon. Followed quickly by clue three, super flirty dancing by herself. In a few minutes, she'd take the bobby pins out of her hair and do the hair flip and comb out her blonde hair with her fingers. Next, she'd start the hip sway and tipsy Brie would be in full effect.

"Brie, it's fine." I shook my head and started to pull out from under her arm.

"By the way, I'm staying at Danny's tonight. He figured it was dumb for me to keep half living there and half with you. He's picking me up soon."

"Awesome. I'll pack your clothes and stuff for you so you can pick it up."

"You're such a sweetie. Thanks! There's not much. We can pick it up tomorrow."

"I work nine to eleven and then I have plans, but I'll have it all packed before I go to work." I thought to myself *I only offered so you didn't "accidentally" take anything of mine. Plus, I want to move the air mattress out of the dining area that I never used as a dining area. I want my art area back.* I grabbed my bag and got ready to head for the door. *I should say bye to Jesse.* I walked over to the bar.

"Hey Lexie, what can I get you?" Jesse asked before I was even up to the bar. His dark brown eyes locked on me as I walked up to the bar.

"Nothing. I wanted to say goodnight. Danny's picking her up. I guess I get my studio back to myself starting tonight. I'm going to go pack her stuff."

"I'm sure you are excited about that. It's not busy. Let me walk you out to your car since you're leaving by yourself." He caught Tony's attention. "I'll be right back. I'm walking Lexie to her car." Tony nodded and we headed to the door. When we got to my car, Jesse opened my door for me. "It was fun catching up with you tonight Lexie. Thanks for hanging out.

I'll see you tomorrow. Drive carefully." He closed my door and turned to start to walk away. Then he turned back and motioned for me to put my window down. "Give me your phone. I'll give you my number. Let me know when you're on your way over tomorrow. I should be there all day unless I need to run to the hardware store." I handed him my phone, he put his number in and then texted himself, so he'd have my number. "Goodnight Lexie."

"Goodnight Jesse."

When I got home, I changed out of my bar clothes that were my sisters and put on my comfy lounge around the house clothes that were more my style. I grabbed boxes and started packing all of Brie's stuff. I was ten minutes into packing when I got a text from Jesse.

Did you make it home safely?

Yes. Now I get to pack. I'm so excited.

Enjoy! I'll see you tomorrow.

When I was done packing Brie's stuff, I set my art studio area up and went through my box of old sketches. I hoped I still had it. I finally found it in an old portfolio. It was faded but other than that it was still perfect. I grabbed a manila envelope and slid it inside and set it in my purse so I wouldn't forget it. Then I crawled into bed.

~ ~

I taught two classes the next morning and had a meeting with the Director working on details for the upcoming summer festival. I wanted to turn the art show into a fundraiser to help raise money for additional classes and maybe expand to start teaching some adult classes. When I was done teaching, I sent Jesse a message.

I'm done. I need to clean up supplies and then I can head over. Let me know when you're home.

I'm home. Come by anytime.

I pulled up and parked in front of the house on the street. Jesse was outside on the ladder in front of the porch. I opened the white wooden gate to the front yard and walked under the ivy-covered arch. "Hi. This place looks great. You picked a paint color that matches almost exactly what I remember from when I was a kid."

"Hey. How was work?" He stepped off the ladder and started to walk toward me. He was in jeans and a plain white t-shirt that clung to his chest. You had to be a complete idiot to not know Jesse was handsome, but slightly sweaty, just spent the morning doing house repair Jesse was hot.

"It was fun. I had two classes with the younger kids today, watercolors and acrylics."

"Nice. And thanks, for the paint color. I was torn but decided that I wanted to restore it to as close to the original light blue as possible. I finished repairing and repainting all the shutters and put them back up this morning. It had a weird, mismatched gray and white trim that I didn't like so I went with the gray trim and did white shutters. I feel like the house is so iconic to those of us who grew up here that instead of completely changing it, I want to honor the past and restore it as closely as I can, but still make it feel more modern."

"I love that idea. It would be so strange to see this house any other color but blue and the fence anything but white. I love that you are keeping it close to the original. I have something for you." I walked toward him and met him in the middle of the pathway from the gate to the front steps.

"What? You didn't have to bring me anything."

I held the envelope out. "Here, open it."

He opened the envelope, pulled the paper out, looked at the sketch, and turned to look at the orange tree. "Wow. Lexie, this is good. When did you do this?"

"My freshman year in high school. We had to do a project for English class and instead of taking a photo to go with my essay. I did a sketch. I thought you might like it."

"I love it. Thank you! Let me give you a tour. This is the orange tree that we all remember from childhood. You have to see this backyard. It's amazing." I followed him through the side yard to the back yard. He was right, it was amazing. There were rows of raised garden beds full of flowers and a small greenhouse.

"Wow. Jesse this back yard is amazing. It's such a small house. I wouldn't have expected such a big yard."

"It gets better. Turn around and look at the house."

I turned and instantly figured out what he wanted me to see. A screened back patio with an art easel. "There's a patio and they used it as a studio. Jesse that space is amazing."

"The walls are covered in sketches and paintings of the flowers in this backyard. I can't bring myself to cover them. I have no idea what I'm going to do with the space, but I know I have to leave the artwork. It's part of the house's history."

I turned back and looked at him. "Can I go see?"

"Of course. Once you said you always thought the front porch would be perfect to paint and sketch at, I knew you'd love this. Go check it out and then I'll show you the rest of the house. I'm going to go move the ladder. I don't want a kid to walk in the yard and climb it and get hurt. I'll be back in a minute."

I went up the back steps and opened the screened porch. *I would love a studio space like this. Wow!* I started at one side of the porch and made my way through to look at all the artwork. I sensed Jesse was there before I heard the screen open or his footsteps. "These are amazing. Do you have a favorite?"

He walked up the three steps and opened the screen. "The purple irises on the end by the window."

I walked over and he was right. That painting was amazing. I examined it a little more. "This is a mixed media piece."

"What does that mean?" He was right next to me.

"More than one type of material was used. It's canvas and linen and there's a mix of watercolor and acrylic paint. The combination is what gives it the texture effect. It's gorgeous." I turned and looked at him. I had almost forgotten how dark his eyes were and they always seemed to be on me even last night at the bar. I could sense when he was looking at me while working behind the bar. "Show me what you've done to the house." He opened the back door and let me in the house.

"I redid the laundry room so that it has a sink and put cabinets in for storage. Since it's only a two-bedroom and one bath, there's not a ton of storage space. I can use the laundry room cabinets for sheets, towels, paper products, and stuff like that freeing up space in the bathroom. I like that the laundry room is right by the back door. It makes it easy when I come home from work to drop my gross work clothes into the wash. I knocked down the wall between the kitchen and living room because I wanted to open the place up and make it feel larger. I added the counter area instead of the wall, so it's still separate but the counter has a purpose. I can eat breakfast there or drink coffee in the morning. I eat there more than at the table since it's just me. I updated the kitchen completely. Not that I cook much, but I do occasionally. I refinished all the floors. It's original hardwood all through the house except the bathroom. I gutted the bathroom and redid that."

"Jesse, this is amazing. It's done, right? It doesn't seem like there's anything left to do."

"Windows. Before winter, Marco and Tony are going to help me replace all the windows. Other than that, it's done besides the decorating stuff which I could care less about. I want a big enough TV to watch games, movies, and play video games on with a comfortable recliner or an awesome couch. Other than that, I don't care. Marco and Tony both have these awesome L-shaped couches that I love so I'm probably going to go with something like that. I need to decide on size and color. Jenna and Gabby say they're going to help me."

"I know Gabby because she takes the acrylic class I teach once a week. She was in my class this morning. Her Grandma picked her up. Is that your aunt?"

He nodded. "Yep. She's my aunt, but she was Mom growing up and still is."

"Jenna? She's Marco's sister, right? She does drop off and pick-up sometimes."

"No. A lot of people think that because she lived with Marco and his mom through the end of high school. Her brother was Marco's best friend. He died in a racing accident about ten years ago. Jenna moved in with Marco's mom because her mom had bailed years before and her dad was awful."

"Sounds familiar."

"What?" He stepped closer to me. "You don't have to tell me if you don't want to." He motioned to the couch and sat on one end and I sat at the other.

"It's fine. My parents divorced when Brie was five and I was three. My mom left right after the divorce and we never saw her again. We had a series of 'live-in babysitters' who were whatever flavor of the week our dad was dating. By age ten, Brie was basically raising us. She moved out at sixteen and Dad told me I could go with her if I wanted, so I did."

"Damn. I don't understand parents who make those decisions. Don't have kids unless you're going to commit to raising them."

"Is that why you don't want kids?" I paused for a moment. "Sorry, I shouldn't have asked that."

"Basically. My mom and dad never married so I bounced back and forth between them based on their ever-changing work schedules and my aunt, Marco's mom, took me the rest of the time. I spent more time there, than anywhere else. She sort of adopts all of Marco's friends and everyone calls her mom. Even though she's my aunt, I don't call her that. She's mom. If I wasn't at her house, I was with Rocky. Rocky's my dad's oldest brother. My dad was the middle and Marco's dad was the youngest, but when it came to responsibility, my dad was the most irresponsible of them, meaning he lacked responsibility completely and they did their best to make up for it. My uncles stepped in and helped raise me. My mom's youngest sister Maria is still a big part of my life. She was too young to help raise me, but she's always been around as an adult to help me when I've needed it. She lives a couple of hours away, so I try to visit at least once a month."

"It's great that you had so many aunts and uncles growing up. We sort of ended up on our own. Marco's mom sounds awesome." I looked up on the wall and saw it. I couldn't believe it. I stood up and walked toward it and then turned to look at him. "You framed it already?"

"I did. I came into the house after putting the ladder up and put it in the frame before coming back out to the studio area. That frame was empty when I bought the house. It was old and I liked it, so I kept it. Your sketch looks beautiful in it and it's perfect by the window overlooking the orange tree."

"I don't think anyone has ever shown as much appreciation for one of my pieces as you. Thanks, Jesse. It means a lot." I turned toward Jesse. "I know you were working on stuff and it's your day off. I should head out. Thanks for showing me the house."

"What are you doing the rest of the day Lexie?"

"Truth or should I give the girly answer?"

"Truth. Always."

"I'm going to order a pepperoni pizza and eat it by the pool at my apartment. I'm celebrating having my apartment back."

"Sounds like a perfect afternoon. Out of curiosity, what would your girly answer have been?"

I used my fake super girly voice. "I'm going to go for a run and then go get my nails done." I did the girly hair flip tossing my hair from over the front of my shoulder to behind my shoulder as I said it. He laughed. "I don't run. Ever. I don't pay for someone else to paint my nails. I'd rather spend that money on pizza." He laughed again.

"Your truthful answer sounds like it's a lot more fun. You can't go wrong with pizza and the pool. Your other plans sound high maintenance and make me cringe."

I laughed. "What else are you doing at the house today?"

"Nothing. It's too hot. I got my to-do list done before the heat. Now the afternoon is for relaxing. I was going to order pizza and play video games."

"I have a better idea."

"What's that?"

"Want to share a pizza, swim, and then play video games at my place?"

"I would love to. I need half an hour to clean up a few things. I can grab a pizza on my way over. Want me to grab drinks too?"

"I have beer and flavored water. If you want anything else, bring it; otherwise, we're all set. I'm in the apartments on Orchard in 7B. I'll text you the gate code." I pulled out my phone from my pocket and sent him the code.

"Let me walk you to your car." He walked me to the car and before shutting my door said, "see you in about forty-five minutes."

Forty-five minutes later there was a knock at my door. I opened it expecting Jesse. "Hey, you're right on time."

"Hey Baby."

"Kyle, what are you doing here? You need to go." I started to push the door closed.

He placed his hand on the door over my head and started to step forward. "Come on Baby. It's been six months; you always forgive me. Let me come in."

"No. I'm done forgiving you. Nothing changed the other two times and I know they won't. I told you that six months ago and again every time you called. I can't do this anymore."

"Lex, don't be like this. You know you love me. I'm sorry. I don't know how many times I can say it, but I'll say it until you believe me. I'm sorry. I'm sorry. I'm sorry." He brought his face down toward mine like he was going to kiss me. His green eyes locked on mine and he started to place his forehead on mine. *I can't believe I used to melt when his eyes locked on me and now all I see is a monster.*

I pulled back and moved my head but kept my hands on the back of the door. "Stop. I don't want to hear it. You need to go. I'm expecting someone. Go."

"What do you mean you're expecting someone?" He started to push the door harder. He was so much stronger than me, I couldn't prevent it. He pushed it open and pushed me out of the way with his left hand as he stepped into the apartment. I fell backward to the wall. As I fell, Jesse was in the doorway.

"What the hell? Sweetheart, are you okay?" He reached his hand out for me. I took his hand and he helped me up. He took his left hand and guided me behind him putting me between him and the open door. He stared at Kyle. "I don't know who you are, but you need to leave." He took two steps forward and set the pizza on the coffee table and then continued to walk toward Kyle. Kyle had broader shoulders and probably weighed thirty pounds more, but Jesse was almost two inches taller.

"Who are you?" Kyle said as he took a step forward.

"I'm the one who was invited and you're the one who is leaving. If you ever place a hand on her again, I will break it. See yourself out, or I will help you leave." Kyle shoved Jesse in the shoulders with both his hands, but Jesse didn't move. "I'll happily kick your ass, but I won't destroy her apartment. Get out or I will show you out."

Kyle walked toward the door. I had moved out of the entryway and was standing against the wall. He paused near me. "Are you sure you want him instead of me? If I walk out, I'm not coming back."

"I don't even have to think about it. Get out." He walked out the door and pulled it shut, slamming it behind him.

Jesse walked to me. "Are you okay?"

"Yeah, I'm fine. That was nothing. Honestly, if I had moved, it wouldn't have happened."

I was standing with my back plastered against the wall. I took a deep breath in and let it out slowly. I was so glad Jesse had shown up. I don't know what I would have done. He placed his forehead on mine and gazed deep into my eyes. "No. First, that was something. That was a man putting his hands on a woman and that should never happen in any circumstance. Second, that was a man pushing his way into a woman's home when she hadn't invited him in. Third, don't take that on yourself by saying 'if I had.' This is all on him."

"Okay," I said quietly and shifted my eyes slightly. I could feel the tears and hoped to stop them before Jesse noticed.

"Are you okay?"

"Yeah, let's not let it ruin the afternoon, alright?"

"Alright." He backed up a bit and I moved past him. "Pizza, swimming, or video games first? It's your choice Gorgeous."

I quickly wiped the tears that had started to form. "Pizza and video games, then swim, then you can decide if you want to get your ass handed to you a second time and play more video games."

He laughed. "Let's do it."

The pizza had been gone for almost an hour by the time we called it even on the video games and we headed to the pool. We swam and hung out at the pool for a few hours. We quickly realized that we are both highly competitive. We raced laps across the pool. He won freestyle, but I took backstroke and butterfly for the championship. I had taken a deck of cards to the pool with us and we found out that we are both good at poker. When a family with five kids came to the pool, we headed back to my apartment for our second round of video games.

While Jesse was changing into dry clothes, I threw double fudge rocky road brownies in the oven. Twenty minutes into our video game, he turned toward me. "Why does your apartment smell like chocolate?"

"I'm baking brownies. I have a huge, sweet tooth and I need chocolate after dealing with Kyle. They'll be ready in about 15 minutes."

"Best day ever! I love brownies. Are you the type of person who eats a tiny square or do you cut a huge piece?"

"Neither. I'm an eat it with a spoon straight out of the pan girl. Preferably while it's still warm and with ice cream."

"Where have you been all my life? You play video games. You can kick my ass swimming. You like poker. You like pizza and beer, and you eat brownies from the pan."

"All of that describes a friend. That's where I've been, in the friend zone, and since you don't do relationships and I only end up with assholes so I'm swearing off men, I think we have could become friends."

"I like it. So, friend, what are you doing next week on Friday night?"

"I teach art classes in the city until four-thirty, so I won't be back in town until between five forty-five and six. Then no plans."

"Well, I'm off at six or six-thirty at the latest. Can I pick you up at seven and take you to a backyard barbecue at Marco's? It will be a small group and we usually end up playing poker toward the end of the night."

"Yeah, I'd like that." The timer went off on the oven. I pulled the brownies out of the oven and set them on the stovetop to cool a bit. "Do you want yours with or without ice cream?"

"The answer is always yes if the question is ice cream." He was right next to me when he said it. "Wow. Those look amazing." I cut him a huge piece put it in the bowl and scooped chocolate chip ice cream on it. He walked back to the couch and sat down. He took a huge bite made a ridiculously exaggerated moaning sound. With brownie still in his mouth, "can you cook food food or just baked stuff?"

"First, baked stuff is food food. Second, one of my grandmas is from Mexico and the other is from Italy. I can cook."

He threw his head back and said, "I might have to reconsider my thoughts on relationships Sweetheart."

"Or don't. Because I swore off men after Kyle." I sat down on the other side of the couch. He reached his arm out and pulled me over to him by the waist.

He lowered his voice slightly. "Not all guys are assholes. Not all guys put hands on women. I'm not a relationship guy because of my own shit. I like the friend idea with you because we have a lot in common. Don't swear off all men if you want a relationship, marriage, kids, the works. You're a great girl. Some guy's going to be lucky to find you."

"Thanks, Jesse. I think I need a break from the assholes."

"More than one asshole in your history?"

"Every guy I've ever dated. What you saw today was nothing."

He shook his head as he stared at me. "Just because it's what you've known doesn't mean all men are like that. You'll find the right one."

"I'm not in a rush. Someday maybe."

"In the meantime, you can cook for me any time when we hang out."

"Deal."

We finished the entire pan of brownies before he left that night. About 20 minutes after he left, I got a text message.

Thanks for a fun day and thanks again for the sketch of the orange tree. See you next Friday. I'll pick you up at 7. Goodnight.

Thanks for today. See you next Friday. Goodnight.

Two days later, I got a text from Jesse around lunchtime.

> *I'm covering the bar tonight from 8 to close. If you stop by, I'll buy you a drink.*
>
> *That sounds fun. I'm done teaching classes in the city at 4:30. What time are you off at the garage?*
>
> *6*
>
> *I have beef stew cooking in the slow cooker. Want dinner before you work?*
>
> *Yes! I'll need to go home and shower before coming over. I can be there 630/45. Do you want me to bring anything?*
>
> *Nope. I've got everything for dinner. I have flavored waters, soda, and beer.*
>
> *See you for dinner.*

He knocked on my door right at 6:30. This time I checked the peephole before opening the door. "Hey, Jesse." He was dressed in jeans and a black t-shirt that clung to his shoulders and chest. Jesse wasn't just hot when he'd been doing house maintenance, he was hot all the time. *This could be trouble.*

"Hi, Gorgeous. Thanks for the invite to dinner." He handed me a pink box from the small bakery near the garage. "I can't bake, but I can order, and Friday's are fancy cupcake days at the bakery. Today's cupcake was chocolate with hot fudge filling and espresso peanut butter frosting. I grabbed two."

"Thank you. That sounds amazing. I love that bakery, but always miss the cupcakes since I get back in town after they close."

"We call when they open on Fridays and find out what the special is and one of us will run over and grab a few. Marco gets cookies or cupcakes for Gabby every Friday unless Jenna is going to be in town for the weekend because then she bakes with Gabby."

"That's super sweet. I set the coffee table for dinner since I don't have an actual table."

"It's perfect. What can I help with?"

"Can you grab a water from the fridge for me and whatever you want? I'll serve dinner. I know you need to be at work at eight."

"I sure can, and I let Tony know that I might be a little late. It doesn't get busy until nine or later. Dinner is more important than covering the bar." He followed me into the kitchen. I grabbed two bowls from the cupboard and started serving dinner.

"Food is more important than work?" I turned and faced him.

He laughed and shook his head. "No. Plans with you are more important than covering when it's still slow." He grabbed two bottles of water from the fridge and headed to the couch.

"I usually eat stew on its own since it has veggies in it, but I have salad stuff if you want a salad," I called to him from the kitchen where I was serving stew.

He was right next to me when he answered. "Stew is perfect. I would have been eating cereal before heading in and then snacking on pretzels, chips, and popcorn for the rest of the night, so this is an amazing treat. Thank you." He took both bowls from me and followed me to the couch. He handed me my bowl and then sat. He took a bite. "This is the best beef stew ever. Don't tell my aunt I said that though. She can cook, but Gorgeous, this is amazing."

"It's super easy. I could teach you and then you wouldn't have to eat cereal for dinner."

"You tell me what I need to buy, and you can come over and give me a cooking lesson one day or we can cook here. Whatever works for you."

"Either, but if we're here, we can swim."

"Swim. Definitely."

We spent the next half hour talking and laughing while we ate. It was seven forty-five when I cleared our bowls and grabbed the cupcakes he brought. "I guess you will only be a few minutes late." We each took a bite of cupcake. "This cupcake is amazing Jesse. Thank you for bringing them."

"You're welcome. Seriously, it was the least I could do after you invited me for dinner. I should be getting ready though. You're still coming by the bar, right?"

"Yeah, I'll head over in a bit. I'm going to clean up the dinner stuff. I'll text Brie to see if she wants to hang out. If not, it will just be me."

He stood up from the couch. "I'll let Rocky know you're coming, so you can go in and you don't have to stand in line."

"It's that the equivalent of a guest list?" I laughed.

"Basically. It gets so busy during the summer. It's weird how busy it gets from June to halfway through August. You shouldn't have to wait to get in since I'm the one who wants you there to hang out while I work."

"Thanks. I'll see you in a little while." I locked the door behind him after he left. I changed into tighter jeans and a cute shirt. I stuck with my checkerboard Vans because I liked them, and they were comfortable.

Rocky saw me walking up before I realized he had. "Hi, Lexie. Jesse told me you were coming by. Go ahead and head in. Is Brie coming?"

"Thanks. No, she and Danny had plans with people from work. He's up for some promotion so they're trying to do stuff with work people in the city on Friday nights now and apparently, he's Daniel now. He says it sounds more professional." I rolled my eyes.

Rocky laughed. "Have fun. Jesse said that the spot at the end of the bar by the wall is yours. He's working that side of the bar and Tony's working the other."

"Thanks." I bypassed the line and headed to the spot at the bar Rocky told me Jesse had saved for me. His eyes were on me as soon as I was halfway between the door and the bar.

He pointed to the spot at the end and I nodded. As soon as I sat down, he asked "what would you like?"

I pulled out my wallet. "Vodka soda with a twist."

He seemed a little surprised. "Put your wallet away. You're on my tab tonight."

"Why do you look surprised by my drink order?"

"Two reasons. First, you usually don't drink when you're driving, and second, it's my favorite drink when I'm not drinking a beer."

"I'll have one drink and then switch to club soda."

He set my drink down in front of me and leaned forward. "I like your plan. It means you stay longer."

I smiled. He set pretzels and popcorn in front of me. "You're joking, there's no way I can eat. We just ate dinner and had fancy cupcakes."

"Habit." He winked at me as he walked over to help the people that walked up to the bar. I stayed for two hours and then headed home. Jesse walked me out to my car. He opened my car door for me. "Thanks again for dinner and for hanging out tonight."

"Thanks for the invite. It was fun. Let me know when you want that cooking lesson."

"I will. Plus, I need a swimming rematch. Text me when you get home and let me know you made it."

"I will. Goodnight Jesse."

"Goodnight Lexie." He shut my door and watched me drive away.

I made it home.

Is your door locked?

Yes.

Thanks again for dinner and for hanging out tonight.

You're welcome. I should have sent you with leftovers. I didn't even think of it until I got home.

That's sweet. You fed me once. I'm good. What are your plans for this weekend?

Swimming, reading, and sketching. What about you?

I work a half-day tomorrow. I ended up needing to cover for Marco last minute so I'm off at noon or one depending on how busy we are. Other than that, nothing. Tony said he might the door covered a couple of hours tomorrow from 5-8. He'll let me know later tonight.

Want to come to swim after work and you can have leftover stew for lunch?

I'd love it. I'll bring stuff to change/shower in case I need to work here, is that okay?

That's fine. See you tomorrow.

Goodnight Gorgeous. I'll text you when I lock up and close. Let me know if I need to bring anything.

Goodnight Jesse.

I got a text from Jesse right after noon the next day.

On my way over. Do you need me to bring anything?

Nope. See you soon.

We spent the afternoon swimming and then finished all the leftover stew. I baked fresh bread that morning to go with it. Jesse had showered after swimming while I heated lunch and set the coffee table. My entire apartment now smelt like cedar and mint, the combination of his body wash and cologne. We were sitting on my small couch eating and playing poker.

"Gorgeous, this meal is even better today. Thank you so much." He took the last of his bread and dipped it into the bottom of his bowl, to get the rest of the stew.

"You're welcome. There's more, do you want another bowl?"

"Yes, please. I can get it though. Do you want more?" He stood up and held his hand out for my bowl.

I shook my head. "No, thanks, but can you slice me another piece of bread."

"I sure can. That bread is amazing too. I can't believe you made it. It tastes like it came from a fancy bakery."

He came back a minute later with bread for me and stew and bread for him.

"Do you have any plans tonight?" He sat closer to the middle of the couch this time instead of right at the end.

I shook my head since I had just taken a bite of bread.

"I have to work the door five to seven, but I have no plans after. Want to head over with me and hang out? I can drive so you can enjoy a drink or two."

"You don't mind?"

"Not at all."

"Sure. That sounds fun."

Jesse insisted on washing dishes after we ate. I got ready and then we headed out. Rocky's wasn't super busy when we got there. Jesse made me my favorite drink and I ran into Brie, so I had someone to hang out with while Jesse worked the door.

"What's going on?" Brie asked when she saw me with Jesse.

"He's kind and he's fun. It's nice to have someone to hang out with who has no relationship expectations. We're friends."

She bit her lower lip like she does when she's holding something back. Then she went for it. "Are you sleeping with him?"

"No. Definitely not. He's a total video game nerd like me. He likes swimming. We've been hanging out."

"Interesting. I never saw Jesse as a friends guy."

I shrugged my shoulders. "When we ran into each other at your bachelorette party we both realized we had a ton in common and we've been hanging out a couple of times a week. I need to get out of the apartment."

She nodded. "Be careful."

"I'm not looking for a relationship and neither is he." I sat with Brie, Danny, and Danny's boring friends until Jesse was done working the door. He brought me another drink and stood between me and Danny's friend who was trying to make awkward small talk.

"Hey, Jesse," Danny said from across the table. "These are my friends from work." Danny introduced Jesse to everyone.

"Nice to meet you." He leaned over to me and lowered his voice so only I could hear. "Our table's open should I go reserve it?" I nodded. He came back a minute later with a bottle of water for him and bowls of chips, pretzels, and popcorn for the table. Once again lowering his voice, "it's ours when we want it."

We hung out with Brie and Danny for another half hour before they decided to head home. We moved to our table even though Danny's friends invited us to stay. "I promised when I was done covering the door, that she'd get my undivided attention." Jesse took my hand and led me to the table.

"Thanks for saving me from Danny's friend. I kept ignoring him and declining offers to buy me another drink, but he wasn't getting the hint I wasn't interested."

"No problem and to be honest, I didn't realize at first that's what I was doing. I didn't want to stand between you and Brie, so I stood on your other side. I didn't fully realize what I had done until I got dirty looks from him, but he can deal with it. If you were interested, you would have already made that noticeable by the time I got to the table."

"Exactly."

We stayed for a couple more hours before he drove me home. He walked me to my door and made sure I locked it before he left. Twenty minutes later I got a text.

Thanks for a great afternoon and night.

Thanks for getting me out of the apartment. Goodnight.

Goodnight. Sleep well.

Thursday night was my sister's third wedding. It was small; thankfully, and there were no complications or fits of drama. It was a simple ceremony followed immediately by dinner. Halfway through dinner, I got a text message.

How was the wedding?

Drama free, which is always a good thing considering my sister's history. We are halfway through dinner. As soon as they cut the cake, I'm out of here.

There's an accident on the back road into town. You're going to have to take the highway in.

Thanks for letting me know. It would have sucked to get stuck sitting there.

You're welcome. Text me when you get home and let me know you made it.

I will.

Two hours later, I was home. I changed into jammies and crawled into bed. It had been a long day and I had to drive into the city to teach in the morning. I grabbed my phone and sent Jesse a message.

I'm home. I'm going to crash because I get to drive back into the city in the morning to teach all day.

I'm glad you're home. Sleep well. I'll see you tomorrow night. I'll text you when I'm off work, so you know when to expect me.

Goodnight.

Chapter 3

Jesse

"**C**an you pick up ice on your way to the house tonight?" Marco asked as we were closing the garage. He armed the building and we walked out the back door. He locked all three locks.

"Yeah, I'll be there around seven-thirty. I need to go shower and change before I pick up Lexie."

He turned toward me. He was two years older than me and since I spent more time living in his house as a kid than anywhere else, he was basically my older brother, more than a cousin. He was almost three inches taller than me, had broader shoulders thanks to all his years playing football, and had close to thirty pounds on me. He was the oldest, tallest, and strongest, out of the three cousins, and took his role as family protector seriously. He pushed his lips together like he does when he's holding something back.

Then shook his head and said what he was thinking. "I still can't believe you're bringing someone. It's been ages since you've dated someone."

"She's not a date. She's a friend. We have a lot in common, but she's six years younger and recently got out of a messed up relationship. Neither of us is looking for a relationship."

"Right. Keep telling yourself that. Tony told me you two hung out at the bar twice last week even on a night you were working."

"Why are you and Tony talking about me?"

"Because it's unexpected and we're cousins who grew up like brothers. It's what we do."

"Hey, if you can be friends with Jenna, why can't I be friends with Lexie?"

He stopped mid-step and stared at me. "Because I've wanted to be more than friends with Jenna since the day I met her. Once she was legal, she lived across the hall from me and Mom would have killed me. It's been a series of bad timings. I'm hoping someday she's mine. I'm not kidding myself that I only want to be friends with her."

"Well, I'm not a relationship guy and Lexie is a relationship girl." I emphasized the word 'is' when I said it. "She's on a break from relationships, so this is perfect."

"If you say so. Let's see, I say by the time Joey is home on leave in a couple of weeks, you'll be a relationship guy."

"Not gonna happen. Want to place a bet?" I looked him dead on when I offered the bet.

"Yep. If you're in a relationship by the time Joey's leave is over, you take two of my Saturday shifts. If you're not, I'll work two of yours."

"Deal. See you in a bit." I jumped on my bike and headed for the house. I parked in the garage and headed into the house to shower and change. I sent Lexie a text.

Marco asked me to grab ice on the way. Do you mind stopping with me? I can get it on my way to you instead.

I don't mind stopping. See you soon.

I pulled into the complex and punched the code into the gate. Lexie told me where closer visitor parking was than where I had parked the other two times I'd been here. I noticed a truck with a familiar figure in it when I pulled into the parking area. I circled through to make sure I was right before I told Lexie. Unfortunately, I was right. Kyle was sitting in her parking lot. He was in the visitor area that wasn't visible from her building by right by the path leading directly to her apartment.

I parked in the spot closest to her building and headed up the stairs to her apartment. I knocked on her door and she let me in. "Hey, how was your day Jesse?" I loved the way my name sounded on her lips which was new for me.

I stepped into the apartment and headed toward the couch. Her place was small, but one hundred percent her. The walls were filled with drawings and paintings of her work. She had a few framed photos of her and Brie from childhood. She maximized the space by using the small nook designed for a table as an art area and had set the couch against the foot of the bed and the dresser against the wall directly across from it to use the dresser as a TV stand and the coffee table served as a coffee table and regular table. There was a bookshelf next to the bed and it served as both a bookshelf and a nightstand. The art area had her painting and drawing supplies on a longer bookshelf and two easels. There was a small two cubby shelf against the wall. Lexie didn't have much outside of the basics. "It was good. How was yours?"

"Traffic in from the city was the pits even getting done as early as I do. I might need to switch up my days and not teach in the city on Fridays. Other than that, it was uneventful, and classes went well."

I sat on her couch and patted the spot next to me. "Come here Sweetheart, I need to tell you something."

"This doesn't sound good." She sat next to me.

I turned toward her. "It's not."

"Are you okay?" I nodded. "Are we okay?" I liked how 'we' sounded which was the first for me. I nodded. "What's wrong Jesse?"

"I saw Kyle sitting in a truck in your parking lot when I pulled in. I circled through to check before telling you."

"Shit. Not again." She turned slightly toward me.

"What do you mean again?" I placed my hands on top of hers in her lap.

"This isn't our first break up. It's our third. The first, I was dumb and took him back believing him right away. The second, he showed up a lot and I was still dumb, I thought it was endearing how he would keep coming back every couple of weeks for months, but I know now it wasn't. It was manipulative and abusive."

"Has he ever sat in your parking lot before?" She nodded. "What did he do?"

Tears formed in her eyes and her voice shook. "Kicked the door in until it opened."

"When did it happen?"

"About two-and-a-half months ago. I paid the fee and got the door replaced."

I reached for her and pulled her to me. I wrapped my arm around her waist. I lowered my voice as I spoke. "Besides the push to the ground I saw, has he ever hurt you? I assume yes, but I need to know."

"Yes. I won't survive that again Jesse. It was so bad." She turned her head into my chest and cried. I wrapped my other arm around her and rested my hand on her back. Her voice shook as she spoke, and she could hardly get the words out. "I don't know what to do. I don't have anywhere else to go. I don't have anyone."

"You have me."

"What do you mean?"

I put my hand under her chin and lifted her head. Her gray-blue eyes locked in on mine. "We're going to the barbecue at Marco's. I have to work tomorrow. It's my Saturday, so you can stay at my house. I have a guest room. Pack some clothes and your art stuff and come use the studio porch. We'll figure out what to do when I get home tomorrow. In the meantime, you'll be safe at my house."

"I can't ask you to do that."

"You didn't ask. I offered. I'm not taking no for an answer. Bring as much stuff as you want. Go grab a bag or box and pack some stuff." I watched as she packed paints, sketching stuff, and clothes. Then she did the unexpected, she walked into the kitchen and packed pantry stuff. "What are you doing?"

"Earning my keep. You're coming home to food food and baked food tomorrow."

"Be careful Lexie, I might not let you leave."

She laughed. "You're ridiculous. He'll lose interest in me after a couple of days. He'll go convince his side piece I was the side piece and she'll take him back. Maybe I was his side piece. I don't know and after over two years close to three years of back and forth with him, I don't even care. I'm done."

"Moron." I meant to say it under my breath or in my head, but I said it at a volume she could hear.

"What?" She turned and looked at me.

I stepped toward her. "Anyone who chooses a side piece over you or chooses to have you as a side piece when they could have everything with you is a moron." I held my hand out to her. "Are you ready?"

"Yeah, let's go." She took my hand, and I pulled her close to my side. I took the duffel bag and backpack from her and put them on my left shoulder. After she locked her door, I put my right arm over her shoulder, pulled her into my side, and walked her to my car. I opened the passenger door for her and made sure she was in before putting her bags in the trunk. We stopped for ice and headed to Marco's.

I parked in my usual spot on the driveway behind his red Honda and next to Jenna's spot. One thing I liked about the older part of town is the lots were big and the driveways were wide. This one was three wide and three deep because Marco's dad had removed most of the side yard when he turned the unattached garage into a shop and extended the driveway to the back of the property.

I got out of the car and opened her door for her. I led her up the front steps to the house. I dropped my keys into the bowl on the entryway table and opened the closet door. "You can put your purse in here. Let's find Jenna and I'll introduce you."

Jenna was in the kitchen with Gabby. I led Lexie across the living room to the kitchen before introducing her to two out of three of the most important women in my life: Gabby, Marco's daughter, who she already knew from art classes; and Jenna, who had almost been my sister and her brother was one of my best friend's until he died almost 10 years ago. Mom was gone for the weekend, so that introduction would have to wait.

"Hi. It's nice to meet you. Gabby and I were working on getting stuff together for dinner. Jesse told me you like to cook. Any chance you can help?" Jenna asked from the kitchen counter where she was prepping dinner stuff.

"Sure. I'd love to. What do you want me to do?" Lexie squeezed my hand slightly before letting go of me as she walked into the kitchen.

"Can you finish making the salad? Marco started and then got distracted by the barbecue. Gabby also hates the dinner tonight and has asked for mac n cheese. Marco usually has a strict eat what's served rule, but I broke it because no five-year-old should be expected to eat kabobs with peppers and onions. I can barely tolerate them myself. Sometimes kids should get fun food. Plus, if we make extra, I can steal some."

"I can take care of both and let's make extra. Mac n cheese should never be considered just kid food."

I stepped into the kitchen and wrapped my arm around Lexie's waist and whispered, "Jenna's amazing. You're going to love her and she's shy too. I need to go talk to Marco. I'll be by the grill." I left them in the kitchen and headed out to the grill to talk to Marco. I needed to find out if he knew anything about Kyle. I walked down the porch steps and crossed the yard to Marco. When I got to the grill, I told him "I think Lexie's got a problem."

"What kind of a problem?" He finished turning the kabobs and then turned to look at me.

"Remember when I told you about her ex?"

He nodded. "The one who entered her apartment by pushing her into a wall?"

"That's the one. When I picked her up tonight, he was parked in her parking lot, but on the side not visible from her apartment."

"You're sure?"

"I circled through to make sure."

"Did you tell her?"

"Of course, I did. I also told her to pack a bag because she was staying with me until I figured out what to do." He gave me the raised eyebrow look he does when he wants to say something, but he's holding it back. "Guest room. I have a guest room. I can't let her stay in her studio. She told me a couple of months ago he kicked her door in."

He let out a sigh and shook his head. "What are you going to do?"

"I'm not sure. Do you know anything about this Kyle guy she was dating?"

"No, but I'm sure Tony does, and he'll be here tonight. Jenna can slumber party in Gabby's room if you and Lexie want to crash here. We can put Lexie in the guestroom, and you can have the couch."

"Thanks, but I think she'll be more comfortable at my house tomorrow while I'm at work. She's going to use the porch art studio."

"Have you decided what you're doing with the patio space yet?"

"Leaving it for now. I don't want to ruin all the artwork. It's part of the house's history. I'm sure I'll eventually move the easel and stuff and put some sort of furniture out there."

"You and Lexie still only friends? Her staying with you after a couple of weeks of hanging out is a leap."

"It's purely because of the circumstance. She's a friend with a problem. I help friends with problems. We hung out on my day off last week and she came into Rocky's the other night and hung out at the bar while I covered a couple of hours. We've been swimming and hanging out at her apartment. We've been texting a lot, but that's it. We're friends."

"Mmm-hmm. Keep telling yourself that." He took a sip from whatever was in his cup. "Let's talk to Tony and find out what he knows about Kyle. See what else you can get Lexie to tell you about him too. Not here of course."

I nodded. "I will. All I know for sure is she's not going back to her apartment until this situation is taken care of."

"Agreed. I don't know her, but I wouldn't want any woman in that situation. You're right. That's what guestrooms are for. Mom will be home Monday and she would have both our asses if she knew we let her go back home to deal with Kyle on her own."

"Where's Mom?"

"She went to visit one of her cousins for a long weekend. By the way, I'm calling this Sunday night dinner because she's not home until Monday. Jenna's already here tonight since she watched Gabby for me when Sonia did a last-minute visit day switch. Gabby will be with Sonia Sunday overnight."

"Works for me. If Sonia bails, let me know and we can throw together a dinner for Gabby even if it's takeout or something."

"Thanks. Tony's here, you should go talk to him while Lexie's still in the house."

I walked over to Tony as he entered the yard from the side fence. "Can I talk to you away from eyes and ears?"

He grabbed a beer from the ice chest at the bottom of the porch steps and walked toward the shop at the back of the driveway. "What's up?"

"What do you know about Lexie's ex Kyle?"

"He's an ass. I'm fairly sure he hit her from the rumors I've heard at the bar. Brie and Lexie have never said anything to confirm it though. It was an on again off again thing for a couple of years. While she was always exclusive when they were on, he never was, but she always thought he was."

"All of it's true. I went to her place last week on Wednesday for pizza and video games and he had pushed his way into her apartment by pushing her against the wall. I made it clear he needed to leave. When I picked her up tonight, he was parked in the parking lot at her complex out of sight from her apartment."

Tony's eyes got wide. "So much to process. First, let me call a friend and find out more about Kyle. Second, are you and Lexie a thing now? I told you"

I cut him off. "We're not a thing. We are friends. She knows I'm not a relationship guy and I know she's sworn off dating because of whatever she went through with Kyle. We have a ton in common and we are friends."

"Be careful. Don't go there unless you're one hundred percent in. She's been like a little sister to me since she was three. I don't care if we are family or not, you hurt her, and I will kick your ass. That's all I'm going to say about it. Let me make a couple of calls." He walked toward the front of the driveway. I headed back into the backyard. I needed to check on Lexie.

I found her in the kitchen with Jenna. "Do you need any help with anything?" I asked as I walked in.

Jenna shook her head. "No, it's super easy. Marco got kabobs ready this morning before he went to work, so I'm doing sides while he has those on the grill. Lexie took care of the salad and is making mac n cheese for Gabby with extra for grownups. I went with easy and made the pasta salad Marco likes. I doubled it so he has it for lunches this week too."

"I'm stealing it when he puts it in the fridge at work."

Jenna peered out the window toward the swing set. "Can you make sure Gabby washes up? I saw Marco pull kabobs off the grill."

"No problem." I headed outside to get Gabby off the swing set and raced her into the house to see who could wash up first. I told her the winner didn't have to help with dishes and clean up tonight. She was as competitive as her dad and never turned down a bet. She won and was happy to know I'd be washing her share of the dishes tonight.

When food was out, Gabby went through the line first, then Jenna and Lexie. Lexie tried to wait, and I told her "In this house, women go first always."

"That's a new one for me. Thanks." She sat down at the table across from Jenna.

I set my plate next to her. "Hey Lexie, what do you want to drink? Beer, margarita, soda, or juice."

"You're driving, so I'll take a margarita unless you want me to drive home tonight."

I brought her back a margarita. She glanced at my soda and smiled. "Thanks."

"You're welcome."

She whispered, "I meant for grabbing a soda since you're driving."

I leaned into her. "I know. I don't mind. I'm usually one or two beers and hours before I drive, but I realize you take the driver doesn't drink rule seriously and I don't mind."

"I appreciate it."

Once dinner was over, we set Gabby up with a bowl of popcorn and a movie and set up the table for the five of us to play poker. Lexie kicked our asses, and it was amazing to watch because Tony and Marco are almost always the last ones standing and it ended up being Lexie and Jenna. After we helped clean up, we headed to my house. About halfway there, she said "crap" under her breath.

"What's up, Sweetheart?"

"I realized I forgot two things. My toothbrush and pajamas. I have shorts I can sleep in but all the tops I brought aren't super comfy for sleeping. I'll figure something out."

"I have a few toothbrushes. The ones you get at the dentist. I don't like the brand, so I throw them in the cabinet. You can have one of those and I'll give you a shirt. Problem solved."

I pulled my car all the up the driveway when I parked. I grabbed her bags from the trunk. "The bottom step out front is loose. I'm going to fix it after work sometime this week, so until then, use the back. I don't want you to get hurt."

"Thanks for letting me know." She followed me to the house and seemed a little surprised when I held the door open for her. *What jerks has she been around that she's not used to getting food first and having doors opened for her?*

"Let's get you settled, and I'll give you a tour of the kitchen. Then I need to head to bed. I have to be at the shop at seven. Thankfully, we are only open until noon, so I'll be home early."

I set her stuff on the guest bed. "The dresser is empty. Feel free to unpack. Put whatever you want to in the kitchen. The bathroom is through that pocket door. It's a walkthrough to my room, so lock my side when you need to, and I'll do the same. I'll put a toothbrush on the counter, and I'll grab you a shirt while you unpack." I went and grabbed a shirt for her. I made sure it was old and soft. I put a toothbrush on the counter and set out the toothpaste. I knocked lightly before entering the room. "I have a shirt for you." I set it on the bed.

"Thanks." She turned toward me. "Let's go check out the kitchen and then you can get some sleep. What time will you be leaving?"

"I'll walk out the door at six-thirty."

I showed her where everything was in the kitchen. I set my car keys on the counter. "If you need to go anywhere, take my car. I know I'm close enough to walk to most places, but I don't want you walking by yourself and no going back to your apartment. I'd prefer you stay here. I can take you anywhere in the afternoon. I'll be home between twelve-thirty and one. I don't want you to feel trapped. I'll take my bike to work. I usually do anyway when the weather's nice."

"Thanks. I will probably need a few things to make food food, but we can go when you get home."

"Perfect. Make a list and we will shop in the afternoon."

She walked to the guestroom and turned back to where I was standing in the kitchen "Goodnight Jesse. Thanks again for letting me stay."

"Goodnight Lexie. You're welcome." I walked through the bathroom to my room. I pulled the pocket door on my side shut and took off my jeans and shirt and crawled into bed. I pulled the gray top cover over me and rolled onto my side.

I usually sleep like the dead and fell asleep as soon as my head hits a pillow. That didn't happen. I couldn't fall asleep. I rolled onto my back and stared at the ceiling. I kept thinking about Kyle and what he had done to Lexie. I didn't know the details, but I knew enough. Tony found out he worked at a sales company in the city and he lived in Mason. He had a reputation of having two to three girlfriends at the same time, and they all thought they were exclusive. He didn't date in his town and never dated girls that lived in the same town at the same time. That's how the girls didn't know about each other. What an ass.

I finally fell asleep a little after four. My alarm went off too early at six. I got ready and headed for the kitchen to get coffee. I was surprised to find Lexie in the kitchen. She was still in my t-shirt. It was long on her and hit right above her knee. It was also huge and sat off her shoulder. Her hair was piled in a bun on top of her head. I liked seeing her wearing my clothes and standing in my kitchen. This was a new feeling for me. "What are you doing up?"

"I made you breakfast and packed food for work. I know it's only a short day, but I figured you'd be hungry."

She had an egg sandwich on a bagel and sliced fruit sitting on the counter for me. A sandwich, veggie slices, and chips were packed and sitting next to the breakfast. I grabbed the egg sandwich and took a bite. "This is delicious. What did you do to make the egg taste so much better than when I make eggs?"

She winked at me. "It's a secret."

I threw the fruit in with the lunch stuff. "I'll eat that when I get to the garage, but I'm finishing this sandwich before I go. I need to start the coffee."

She smiled and handed me my thermos. "Already done. It's black. I wasn't sure what you added."

"It's perfect. I don't use anything. Thank you for all of this. You didn't have to. You could have slept in."

She started washing the pan she cooked the egg in at the sink and looked over at me. "I don't sleep much ever. I got a couple of hours."

"Thanks again. I'll see you this afternoon. Call me if you need me. I'll take you to the store when I get home. Lock the screen and the door after I leave. The front is already locked and bolted."

"Okay." She followed me out the back door and locked up. I noticed her art stuff was already set up on the back porch. I had a feeling she was spending her day there.

Chapter 4

Lexie

After Jesse left, I took advantage of the back porch to paint. The light was amazing so early in the morning. I liked the mixed media iris piece that the previous owner had done and wanted to try the watercolor and acrylic layer technique. The crab apple tree in the back corner of the yard was in bloom. The white and pink flowers were perfect for this project. I sketched the tree and blooms using watercolor pencils, then I would use both watercolor paints and acrylic paints to paint over and fill in, focusing mostly on the watercolors, and using the acrylics to add texture. Right when I finished the sketch, I got a text from Jesse.

> *Thanks again for breakfast and for packing a lunch. Hope your day's going good.*
>
> *It is. I'm painting your crab apple tree.*

I can't wait to see it. Do I get to keep it?

If you want it. It's yours.

I'll want it. See you in a couple of hours.

See you soon.

I added the first layer of watercolor paint and decided it needed to completely dry. I went into the kitchen and started taking inventory of what he had and what I'd need. I threw brownies in the oven so those would be ready when Jesse got home from work. When I was done, I did some watercolor touch up to the painting before pulling the brownies out of the oven. I headed into the guestroom to clean up and change. I got a text from Jesse as I was getting out of the shower.

Leaving the garage now. I'll be home in about 15. I just need to shower and change. Then I'm yours for the rest of the day. Food shopping and whatever else you want to do.

See you soon.

I threw on white shorts, a light blue tank top, and a pair of white sandals. I had just finished putting my hair in a side fishtail braid when I heard his motorcycle. I went out to the porch to unlock the screen door. He was at the bottom step by the time I made it to the door. "Hey, Gorgeous. How was your day?"

"Relaxing. I got the crab apple tree piece started. The watercolor portion is done. I need to add texture using acrylics. I'll do it once it's completely dry."

He walked over to the piece to see it. "It's beautiful. I love it. I need to do an oil change on my car tomorrow, so you can finish it while I do that unless you do it later today."

"I'll do it tomorrow. I have a surprise for you in the kitchen." I opened the door and walked into the house.

"I hope it's chocolate." He took his boots off outside the door before walking in.

"It is."

When he saw the brownies on the counter, he grabbed a spoon from the drawer and held it out to me, and grabbed another for himself. He scooped a spoonful and made that same moaning sound he had at my apartment. "Amazing. They're still warm."

"Pulled them out of the oven about 15 minutes ago." I took a spoonful from the opposite corner, ate it, and rinsed my spoon.

"You're only eating one bite? You know you want more. I'm planning on eating this entire row, before taking a shower and then I can take you to the store. You should eat more brownies. You know you want to."

I scooped another bite. "So good. Why can't we live off brownies?"

"I could. Brownies and ice cream would get me through the week at home and I can steal lunch from Marco. Jenna always sends him too much for the week."

"What's their story are they dating or just friends? The house is filled with her pictures. You told me that she lived there for a while."

"Long story. We met when she was 12 through her brother. Ricky and I were 14, and Marco was 16. Ricky died in a racing accident when Jenna was 16. Jenna's mom was long gone by then and her dad was awful. Marco's mom took her in, and she lived there until she was 20 and got her place in the city so she's close to work. She and Marco have both always wanted more but neither acted on it. It's been a series of bad timing. Ricky's death was hard on Jenna and she's a completely different person now. She used to be as wild as us and super social. Now she's shy, quiet, and takes time to get to know. She reads like you do though, so you have that in common."

"She's nice. I think we could end up friends one day. We both need time."

He finished the last bit of brownie from his row and moved to the sink to wash his spoon. "I'm going to go shower because I smell like grease and then I will be ready to take you anywhere you need to go. Did you think of anything you need besides food?"

"Shampoo."

"We'll grab that too. Give me 10 minutes and I'll be ready."

I finished some clean up in the kitchen and packed the brownies away. He was ready in six minutes. He stood next to me. "By the way, I gave Tony your gate code. He's going to drive through and see if Kyle is still hanging around. Marco will drive through later. We figure if the three of us rotate, he won't notice if he is there. Marco also has multiple vehicles, so it won't be the same one each time and I'll grab one of his so I'm not always in my car."

"You don't have to do that. He'll eventually lose interest."

"It wasn't a question of can we. It was a notification that we were doing it." He took three steps forward to where I was standing against the kitchen doorframe. He placed his forehead on mine and his right hand on the wall over my head. He lowered his voice. "Sweetheart, he's not going to lose interest unless he knows you've moved on and are taken care of by someone else. Me being at your place was a challenge. I knew that when he tried to push me. I thought he'd come to me, not you. I'm going to make sure he moves on for good and until then, you're here."

"I can't ask you"

He interrupted me. "I wasn't asking. This is what we're doing. You're staying here until Marco, Tony, and I have made sure that he's gone. I will tell you that if he puts his hands on me again, I will kick his ass and if he puts his hands on you again ever, I will end him. Real men don't put hands on women. Ever."

I'd never had any man in my life that I could trust or feel safe with. Jesse was different. I did something I've never done before; I made the first move. I raised myself onto my tiptoes, placed my right hand on his shoulder and I kissed him. He leaned in and deepened the kiss. I wrapped my other arm around his shoulder and pulled him to me. He took a step forward and wrapped his left arm around my waist pulling me to him. He parted my lips with his tongue, and I let him in. He massaged my tongue with his and guided me gently back to the wall as he stepped forward pinning me between him and the wall. He slowed us and started to pull away, I whimpered and pulled him back to me.

"Slow Sweetheart, we're taking this slow." He took my hands in his and guided me to the couch. He sat and pulled me to his lap. "I know I made it clear that I'm not a relationship guy and you made it clear that you've sworn off men, so we were both happy with a friendship and someone to hang out with. What just happened was amazing but wasn't something either of us was looking for. We need to talk because I don't think I can just be friends with you, but I don't know how to be in a relationship. I'm sort of at a loss here."

"Let's take it slow. Here's what I need, tell me if it will work for you. I need to be the only girl you have your hands, lips or other body parts on. That's the only thing I need that's different than what you've already been doing."

"I can do that."

"Then let's just keep doing what we're doing and see what happens and talk about anything that's not working and see if we can fix it. I don't think either of us is looking to rush into anything. I did like kissing you and would like to keep doing that."

"I liked kissing you too." He leaned forward and kissed me. This kiss was shorter and gentler than before. He stopped us. "We should go to the store before I have a hard time going slow."

He led me through the house, out the door, and to the car. He walked around to the passenger side and opened the door for me. Once I was in, he closed the door. This is something new that I'm going to have to get used to. Right before we got to the street my apartment was on, I said "Jesse, if I'm staying longer, I need more clothes. I only brought a couple of things."

"Let's swing in and grab more. Get enough for a week and you can wash stuff if you need to. Will that work?"

"Perfect."

He pulled into the complex, punched the code in the gate and we both saw the truck. Jesse drove to the visitor space closer to my building and got out. He looked around before opening my door. I noticed he had grabbed his cell phone from his pocket when he got out of the car. He slid it back in his pocket when he opened my door. "I sent Marco and Tony a message letting them know he's here. We're going to grab stuff and get out. Do you need anything besides clothes?"

"Since I'm here, I'll grab my shampoo and stuff too. Other than that, I'm all set."

"Okay, let's go. Give me your key Sweetheart." I handed him my key and he put his arm over my shoulder and pulled me in close. He unlocked the door and held it open for me. I grabbed my weekender bag from the closet and filled the side pockets with all my bathroom stuff. Then I walked through the apartment to my dresser and started grabbing what I needed. Jesse was standing by the window so he could watch for Kyle.

"I'm just getting a few more things. I'm almost done."

"Get whatever you need. Marco's already in the parking lot. If Kyle shows up, I just have to call him. We scared the shit out of Jenna's ex with our words, that's our plan with Kyle unless he gets physical. We're hoping he stays in his truck like he has been so far. That way I can get you out of here before Marco talks to him."

"I feel bad. This isn't your problem to solve."

He left his spot by the window, walked over to me, put his arm around my waist, and pulled me in close. "I want to solve this for you. You shouldn't have to hide from him. Your home should be safe." He brushed his lips lightly across mine. "Finish packing." He returned to his spot by the window and I finished packing. When I was done, he took my bag from me and locked my door. He put his arm over my shoulder and pulled me into his side as we walked down the steps. Marco met us at the bottom of the steps.

"Here's the keys to the blue Honda. We can switch back later today or tomorrow. I know your car needs the oil changed. I can do it for you if we don't get switched later today." He and Jesse switched keys. We walked to the guest parking and Marco walked the path toward the lot where Kyle was parked. Jesse opened the passenger door for me and then put my bag in the trunk. When he got in the car, he took my hand in his and rested it on his knee. "Groceries, then home. You can paint or sketch or you can kick my ass in video games again."

"Let's get groceries, then I'll prep dinner stuff if you want to go switch cars back."

"I'll keep this until tomorrow. Six hours away from you was enough for today."

"Okay. Our plan is groceries, dinner prep, and video games."

"Sounds like the best way to spend the day Sweetheart."

"As long as there's more kissing." I looked over at him as I said it.

He leaned across the front seat at the red light and kissed me sweetly. "There will be more kissing."

"Good because I like kissing you."

"I like kissing you too. Let's plan on a lot of kissing as soon as we get home."

"I like that idea, Jesse."

We bought six bags of food because Jesse couldn't decide what he wanted out of the options I gave and I was going to be there longer now, so I would have time to make it all. When we got home, he unpacked all the groceries while I unpacked all my clothes and bathroom stuff. While I was unpacking, he came in and stood near the end of the bed. "The bathroom cabinet closest to your bathroom door is empty. You can put all your stuff in there. Put whatever you want in the shower too. Make yourself at home. I want you to be comfortable here."

"Thanks, Jesse. I am comfortable here. I know it sounds weird because I've been here for less than a day, but this feels more like home than my place has felt in months." I stepped toward him and he reached his arm out for me. As soon as I was close enough, he pulled me in and wrapped me in his arms.

"I'm going to make sure you are safe again Sweetheart. I'm going to need some time. Until then, you're here. Now finish unpacking and then I'll help you prep dinner stuff so we can spend the rest of the afternoon kissing." He kissed me sweetly before breaking our embrace so I could finish unpacking.

I found him in the kitchen when I was done. He had started salad prep. "I figured salad goes with anything you decide you want to make."

"What do you want me to make?"

"Everything you planned for the week sounds amazing. What's your favorite?"

"Eggplant parmesan. I can make it with angel hair pasta."

"That sounds so good. Can you please make that?"

"Do you want extra sauce on the pasta, or do you want it with butter, garlic, herbs, and parmesan cheese?" I started pulling things from the fridge and pantry and setting them on the counter.

"Both sound delicious. How do you like it?"

"The garlic butter sauce with extra parmesan is my favorite."

"Let's make that. How can I help?"

"You slice and chop, I'll sauté and get everything going. The pasta only takes a few minutes to cook, so I can cook that while you set the table. Once everything's in the oven I'm sure we can find something to do with our time."

He wrapped his arms around my waist and rested his chin on my shoulder. "Kissing. The answer is kissing."

"That's the answer I was hoping for." I turned my head to the side and kissed him quickly before continuing dinner prep.

Chapter 5

Jesse

As soon as she put dinner in the oven, I pulled her over to the couch. I guided her onto my lap. I rested my hands on her lower back while we talked. "Now we kiss until dinner's ready, but I do need to talk with you first. I want you to know, I'm not expecting anything but kissing to happen. We're going slow. We decided to be more than friends and see what happens, but nothing else is happening while you have no other choice but to be here. I don't want you to feel like you have to."

"I know that you don't expect it and I appreciate that. I'm not ready. I think you realize how messed up things were with Kyle. I'm going to need some time."

"Everything at your pace."

She moved her hands from her lap to my shoulders. "And if I decide I want more than kissing?"

"Tell me or show me and we can talk about it. I'm an open book and I'd rather get it out in the open. No games. Ever."

"I like that. Anything else?"

"Not unless you have anything else you want to talk about."

"Nope, I'm ready to not talk until dinner is ready."

I placed one hand behind her head and guided her forward and pressed my lips over hers and placed the other hand on her side to guide her to rotate slowly on my lap. I took her parting her lips as permission to gently slide my tongue into her mouth. My hand slid down her back and stopped at the small of her back. My other hand that had been on her side was resting now on her thigh. I moved both hands to her butt, one on each cheek, and guided her further into my lap. She wrapped her arms around my shoulders. She ran her fingers up and down the back of my neck and across my shoulders as we kissed. My right hand moved back to the small of her back and my left hand was twisting the end of her side braid. In so many ways this was the most innocent kiss I had experienced in years. There was something amazing about knowing that all we were doing was kissing. I was able to slow and enjoy each moment instead of rushing through the kissing to get somewhere else. Don't get me wrong, I love the other stuff, but nothing I had done with anyone gave me the reactions I got from kissing Lexie. Every soft whimper or moan she made sent a jolt through me and I had to use all my self-control not to rush through this and push her toward the next step. I had no guarantee we would get the next step and I wanted to burn every moment I did have into my memory, because this right here, was the best thing I'd experienced all my life.

The oven timer startled us both. "Wow. I didn't realize we'd been kissing for almost an hour." I whispered to her as we separated.

"About 40 minutes. I set the timer, so we'd have enough time to make pasta."

"Five more minutes? Please." I put five minutes on the timer on my phone and set it next to me. I repositioned us and we kissed. When the timer went off, I said "How about five more minutes?"

"You're bad. We're going to end up with burnt dinner. We'll take a break and then we can kiss after dinner."

"Deal." I kissed her quickly before I guided her up to her feet. "I'll finish salad stuff and set the table."

"Perfect. I'll finish the rest and serve plates."

"What do you want to drink? I have beer, soda, and orange juice."

"Beer."

I was going to have a hard time letting her leave in a few days and that was a whole new thought for me. I don't invite girls back to my house, ever, and now that I have, I can't imagine coming home and not having her here.

"Best meal I have ever eaten. Thank you! That was amazing." I cleared plates and leaned down to kiss her before taking her plate. She joined me in the kitchen and started packing leftovers. She pulled out small containers and started by putting the pasta in the container and added the eggplant. "You could have covered it with foil and put it in the fridge."

"I'm packing individual meals so we can reheat as we want them, or you can take them to work."

"You're sweet. Thank you. Now go relax while I wash dishes. The chef doesn't wash dishes."

"I'm not arguing with that rule. I love to cook, but I hate dishes."

She walked out of the kitchen and into her room. She walked back out about ten minutes later. She had changed and had a book in her hand. "What are you reading Sweetheart?"

"You're going to laugh at me."

I shook my head. "Never."

She sat on the couch and positioned so she could see me at the sink. "*A Walk to Remember.*" I lost it. I busted up. "I told you that you'd laugh."

"I'm not laughing at you, I promise. It's a hilarious story about Jenna and Shauna. Jenna has a rule that she has to read a book before she watches a movie."

"I have the same rule, but didn't know about this book until now, so I'm playing catch up."

"I knew you and Jenna would get along." I finished washing the dishes. I dried my hands and headed into the living room to join her on the couch.

"Tell me the rest of the story. I interrupted you."

"Jenna reads the book. She and Shauna go see the movie. Jenna is pissed because the movie took so many artistic liberties and ruined the book. A year goes by and Shauna chooses the movie for movie night. Jenna forgets that she hated the movie and ends up watching it three more times that weekend. Marco, Joey, and I figure out what movie has been on repeat in the house and tell her that she's lost all credibility for choosing movies and giving movie critiques. Now whenever we have movie nights and no one chooses something in a reasonable amount of time, one of us will mention Nicholas Sparks and the girls request *A Walk to Remember.*"

She laughed. "That's funny and Jenna's right, the book, and movie are too different." She set the book down on the coffee table and crawled across the couch closer to me. I reached my arm over to her and pulled her to me. She lowered her voice to just louder than a whisper. "What do you want to do now that dinner is done, and the dishes are washed? Video games?" I shook my head. "A movie?" I shook my head. "Hmmm, what else is there to do Jesse?"

I whispered in her ear. "Kissing. I'm spending the rest of the night kissing you." I took her lips with mine and placed my hands on her waist guiding her into my lap. Forty-five minutes later, my phone rang. Without breaking our kiss, I glanced at the caller ID. I slowed us to a complete stop. "It's Marco. I need to take this. I'll be right back." I hit answer and put the phone to my ear as I lifted her off my lap and onto the couch next to me.

"Hey, Marco. Give me a second." I muted the phone before telling her "don't go anywhere. I will be back to kiss more in a couple of minutes." I unmuted the phone and stepped outside on the front porch.

"Hey, how'd the talk go?"

"I told him that he needed to leave and that she wouldn't be talking to him anymore. He got out of his truck, pushed me in the shoulders, I'm assuming the same way he did to you and I told him the next time he placed hands on me, I'd be breaking his hands. I also told him the next time he laid a hand or other body part on Lexie, we'd end him. There was a lot of yelling, but he stormed off and left in his truck. Tony let me know he's at Rocky's sitting at the bar bitching about the asshole who stole his girl and the bigger asshole who confronted him this afternoon. He doesn't know we are related or that we are related to Tony. I was thinking about going over there. Want me to pick you up? I'll be there in fifteen minutes."

"See you in a few minutes. I need to let Lexie know what's going on."

I walked back into the house locking the door behind me when I closed it. The couch was empty. "I told you to stay where you were. Where'd you go?" I walked toward her room. I found her throwing stuff in her bag. "What's going on? Why are you packing?"

"I can't let him hurt you."

"What are you talking about?" I walked toward her and pulled her into my arms. "Tell me. Please." She handed me her phone.

> I'm going to find out who he is. I don't appreciate his friend talking to me. You belong to me. As for broken hands and ending me, they have it wrong. I'll be the one breaking and ending.

She started to back away from me. "This is why I can't stay. You can't get hurt because of me."

I pulled her in closer and placed my forehead on hers. "Sweetheart, he's not going to hurt me. I was coming in to tell you that Marco and I know where he is. He's at Rocky's and he doesn't know Tony's our cousin. Marco's on his way to pick me up. We're going to talk to him. All three of us together. This ends tonight."

She pulled me closer to her and squeezed her arms around my waist. She was shaking. "You don't understand how bad it can get. He's strong."

I kept my voice low and calm. "So are we. He's one person. There are three of us." I placed a kiss on top of her head and wrapped my arms around her.

"He will punch, kick, and knee. He fights dirty." Tears were running down her face and her voice trembled as she spoke. "I don't want you to get hurt."

I lifted her chin, so she was looking at me. "The fact you know these things makes my decision even easier. I'm going. I'm not planning on fighting him. I'm going to have a conversation with him. I won't lay hands on him unless he lays hands first. You can't live every day scared of him. We are going to talk. We will see what happens from there. Stay here. Don't leave. I'll be back." I kissed her and left her standing by the bed unpacking.

Marco and I walked past the line of people waiting to get in and up to the door. Rocky let us in, and we ignored the comments. We were family. We don't wait in line. We found Kyle sitting at the end of the bar. Marco stood on his right. I stood on his left. He didn't look at us when we first walked up. I leaned on the bar and lowered my voice so only he could hear me. "I heard you're trying to find out who I am because you have a message for me that you're the one doing the hand breaking and ending." He started to speak. I stopped him. "I wasn't done. You're going to listen to me. She's not yours. Women don't belong to men in the way you seem to think they do. You lost the right to call her your girl when you started fucking someone else. Once she wasn't your only, she wasn't yours at all. She made it clear six months ago you were over and two-and-a-half months ago after you kicked in her door and laid hands on her. That will never happen again because I won't allow it. Is she mine in the sense that she's the person I take care of and protect? Abso-fuckin-lutely. Is she mine in the sense that I control where she goes, who she sees, or what she does with her body? No. Those decisions are only hers. That last one seemed to be a hard one for you to understand, so let me explain it to you. She can see who she wants to see, and she chose me. She can choose what she does with her time and she chose to spend time with me. She can choose what she does with her body and it's none of your fuckin' business. As for breaking my hands or ending me, not going to happen."

I reached over and took his phone. Dumbass doesn't have a passcode on it. I scrolled to her contact and saw photos I'm sure she doesn't know he's taken. Jackass. I deleted all his text message history with her. I deleted her contact information and because I know that douchebags like him have photos of girls on their phones that girls don't realize they've taken, I deleted all his photos because I wasn't scrolling through five thousand photos. I'm not technology stupid like he seems to be, I deleted all his cloud backups and all other file backups. In case I missed anything, I factory reset his phone. He didn't let this happen without a struggle, but Marco is six inches taller and weighs about thirty pounds more than Kyle. That's a lot of pressure on your body when you're being held down on your barstool. "Goodnight Kyle. You don't have any reason to be in Woods Lake anymore. You can see yourself home. The next time we see you, we won't be as nice."

As soon as Marco took his hands off Kyle's shoulders and stopped leaning on him, Kyle started yelling at Tony. "How can you let that happen in your bar?"

Tony leaned across the bar and got less than an inch from Kyle's face. "Easy, Lexie's like a little sister to a lot of us and they're family. You're in a small town and we handle our own business. You laid hands on her. You made her feel unsafe in her own home. You kicked in her door. That. What happened right now, is a lot nicer than anything that I would do to you. I have a feeling Lexie asked him not to kick your ass. She's just done with you. You need to move on."

He stormed out and after us as we were headed for the door. "How long has she been fucking you?" He stepped in front of me. "Answer the question." I kept walking. "She belongs to me." I looked at Marco, he nodded his head, and we each stepped forward and grabbed Kyle by his shoulder and arm and dragged him out the door.

Rocky stood to let us pass. "Good job taking out the trash boys."

We walked Kyle to his truck. I leaned against him pinning him to the side of his truck with my body. "I don't think you heard me the first time. She can choose what she does with her body and it's none of your fuckin' business. She's not yours. Women don't belong to men in the way you think they do. Is she mine in the sense that she's the person I take care of and protect? Abso-fuckin-lutely. Do I make myself clear?" He tried to kick with his feet the way Lexie warned me he would. "Oh no, you don't asshole. I heard about this. Lexie warned me that you knee, kick, and punch and that you fight dirty."

Marco let out a growl. "What? You left that piece of information out. I knew he laid hands on her. I thought you meant how he pushed her to get into the apartment. If he kneed, kicked, or punched her, ever, I'm gonna have fun kicking his ass tonight. Kyle, you have two choices. One, get in your truck and leave and don't ever come back or two, get your ass kicked the way you've been kicking Lexie's and then leave. Either way, you're not coming back. Stay away from Lexie. Stay out of her parking lot. Stay away from her apartment."

"The bitch isn't worth this bullshit. She's boring in and out of bed. Good luck." He stepped to his truck and got in.

"Wrong, so wrong," I said under my breath.

"What's wrong, so wrong?" Marco asked. "Should we have kicked his ass? I thought you said Lexie didn't want us to."

"Oh, I wanted to but promised I wouldn't unless he laid hands first. No, what he said about Lexie being boring. She's amazing Marco. She is artistically talented. She's beautiful. She can cook. I get more from kissing her than I have from doing anything with anyone else."

"Get your ass home and go kiss her and you should tell her all of that. It doesn't seem like she's had anyone in her life who treated her well. Let's go."

As soon as we pulled into the driveway, I saw her. She was sketching on the back porch. She saw me and ran for me. She jumped into my arms. I lifted her by her thighs and guided her to wrap her legs around my waist. "I was so worried about you. What happened? Are you okay?"

"I'm fine. We didn't lay hands on him. We had a discussion. We escorted him to his truck. I pinned him against his truck and made a couple of things very clear to him. First, he kept saying that you were his and I told him that he lost the right to call you his girl when you were no longer his only. He asked how long you'd been sleeping with me. I didn't correct him that you weren't because it's none of his business. I told him you can choose what you do with your body and it's none of his fuckin' business. I also made it clear women don't belong to men in the way he thinks they do. The last thing I told him is you're mine. In the sense that you're the person I take care of and protect. You are abso-fuckin-lutely mine." She kissed me. I lifted her and she wrapped her legs around my waist, and I carried her into the house and sat on the couch. "Can we spend the rest of the night kissing now, please?"

She answered by kissing me long, hard, and deep. "Thank you for taking care of me and for giving me somewhere safe to be. I guess I can go home tomorrow."

I shook my head. "Stay the week and let me make sure he stays away. I'll feel better. We can go get your car tomorrow though."

"I'll stay."

"Best decision ever." We kissed for about an hour on the couch. She started to fall asleep on me, so I scooped her up and carried her toward the bedrooms. Part of me wanted to carry her to my room, but I was enjoying slow and knew that she needed to take things slow. I wasn't going to rush this. As I stepped through her door, she shook her head. "No, what Sweetheart?"

"I don't want to sleep alone. I'm not ready for sex, but can you either sleep in here with me or can we sleep in your room?" I nodded and carried her into my room. I pulled the covers down and placed her in my bed. I crawled in behind her and pulled her to me. I wrapped my arms around her and for the first time, I slept with a woman in my arms.

Chapter 6

Lexie

I woke up on Sunday morning wrapped in Jesse's arm and his leg was over mine pinning me down. *Not a bad way to wake up.* I ran kisses across his chest and up his neck. I heard a low moan followed by a whisper. "Good morning Sweetheart." He brought my chin up to him and leaned in and kissed me sweetly.

"Good morning. Thank you for everything you did last night." I placed my head in that perfect spot on his chest between his shoulder and neck.

"You're welcome. Thank you for trusting me and telling me."

I scooted in closer to him and rotated so I was on my right side and put my left arm across his abs. "Do you have to work today?"

He shook his head. "I need to switch cars with Marco and do the oil change on my car. We need to go get your car too. Do you have anything?"

"I should decide on some lessons for classes this week, but that's it. The community center I teach in the city is doing a two-week full-day camp and I'm not working that since I have commitments to teach here, so I only have my classes here in town. The next two weeks are pretty light, which is nice because I finally have time for some of my pieces and I want to work on the end of summer art exhibit pieces. I figured I can focus on my stuff while you're at work this week since I only have classes a couple of hours a day."

"Sounds like a great plan. What do you want to do today when I'm done with the oil change?" He pulled me in closer to him.

I looked up at him. "You owe me a video game tournament."

"Sounds perfect. When's the last time you had your car's oil change or did a tune-up?"

I shrugged my shoulders. "I'm not sure. I go by the little sticker in the window."

"I'm checking your car out today too."

"You don't have to."

"I wasn't asking for permission. I was letting you know what I'm going to do."

"Let's go get the car swap stuff done. You can get started and I'll make a late breakfast and you can eat between working on the cars. That way you're done before it's hot."

"Sounds perfect. Do you need anything else from your apartment?"

"Nope."

We swapped cars with Marco first, giving him back his Honda and picking up Jesse's. We stopped at my complex and got my car. We both saw Kyle's truck in the visitor spots closest to my apartment. Jesse took my hand and squeezed it. "Damn. I thought we had taken care of things last night, but I guess not. He's not in his truck which is both good and bad since we don't have to see him, but we don't know where he is."

"I'm sure he's at my door and probably kicked it open which means he's destroying the place."

"I'm going to park. You're going to get in your car and drive back to the house. I'm calling Tony and Marco. I'm not going to your place until one of them is here, but we will make sure your apartment is secure."

"I can go with you."

"Absolutely not. Get in your car and drive to my place. Here's the key." He took the house key off his key ring and gave it to me. "I'll call you when I get eyes on your apartment, but I'll wait for Marco or Tony."

"Okay." I gave him a quick kiss before getting in my car and driving away.

Forty minutes later my phone rang. "Are you alright?" I didn't even say hi.

"Yeah. Tony got here first, and we went and checked your apartment. You were right, he kicked the door in again. We got in touch with your apartment manager and they couldn't get anyone out with a door until tomorrow, so Marco picked one up and is on his way with it. We're going to take care of that now."

"Did he destroy everything?"

"Not everything. He did break stuff, but we took photos and I'm getting it cleaned up. Your apartment manager is filing charges."

"Was he there when you got there?"

"Yes."

"Did anyone get hurt?"

"None of us. Your apartment manager had him escorted off the property. We didn't lay hands on him. I promise none of us are hurt."

"Okay. I'll see you when you get home."

An hour later, I heard his car. I heard his footsteps up the back steps and the back door open. "I'm home."

"I know. I heard you. I'm made an extremely late breakfast, so I'm calling it brunch to make it fancy." He came into the kitchen and grabbed me around the waist.

"I'll eat anything you make for me anytime. Thank you. I missed you."

I threw my arms over his shoulders. "I missed you too." I softly kissed him. "First brunch, then more kissing."

He pulled me in closer to him. "A little kissing first, then brunch, then more kissing."

"Deal." He backed me toward the wall and pinned me between him and the wall. I softly nibbled at his bottom lip and he moaned a low moan before letting me go.

"Sweetheart, I could kiss you all day."

"I wouldn't complain about that." I grabbed our plates from the counter and put them on the table. He grabbed coffee for each of us adding creamer to my cup before filling them with coffee.

I had made homemade sausage gravy over biscuits and egg and veggie scramble. "This smells amazing. Thank you."

He took a bite and let out the exaggerated moan that had become his routine.

"You're welcome. Want to tell me about what happened at my apartment?"

"I have the pictures to show you. The apartment manager filed a police report. Kyle knocked everything over and dug through drawers and things. It almost looked like he was looking for something."

"Probably the necklace he gave me. I threw it away along with everything else he ever gave me. He was probably looking for those things and any pictures, but that stuff is all long gone."

"I cleaned up what I could and anything I didn't know where it went, I put in a box and left it on the coffee table. I'll help you when you go over there next. We replaced the door and added a metal security screen door as well. There's no way he's kicking that down or getting in any more. I have two sets of keys for you. The silver is the regular door and the other one is the security door." He set the two sets of keys on the table.

"Speaking of key, I have the door key you gave me." I went to reach for it in my pocket.

He stopped me. "Keep it. You're staying all week. You need keys. If I don't get the front step fixed today, I'll do it tomorrow after work. In the meantime, keep using the other door."

"Okay."

When breakfast was over, he cleared the table and started to wash dishes. I walked in and wrapped my arm around his waist. "I know you have the chef doesn't wash rule, but let's break it. You go take care of cars. I'll clean the kitchen. It's going to be hot later today."

He wrapped his arm over my shoulder and pulled me into him. "Only this once. I'll go do the oil change on my car and figure out what needs to be done on yours. Are you coming out to the studio when you're done here?"

"Of course, I am."

"See you out there." He bent down and kissed me. I finished the dishes he had started, got the kitchen wiped down, and set up everything in the living room for our video game tournament later. Then I headed out to the porch to sketch.

I sat down and started to work on the piece I had started before Jesse got home last night. He was working on his car. When he was done, he came closer to the screened porch. "Let me know if you need me to turn the music down."

"Up would be good. I love *Gin Blossoms*."

"Will do. I just finished my oil change. You need one and a full tune-up and brakes. I don't have everything here to do everything you need. Can I drive your car to work tomorrow? I'll leave you mine, then I can do it at work."

"You don't have to."

"I know, but I want to."

"We can switch cars tomorrow."

"Then I'm done."

"What?"

"I'm going to do everything at work tomorrow. It will be faster with help. I'm going to put stuff away and take a shower. After that, I am all yours for the rest of the day for whatever you want to do."

"Sounds great."

"How's your sketch coming along?"

"I like the way it's turning out. I think it's one I'm going to show. It might even be the piece I put in the auction."

"That's great." He finished the cleanup from working on his car and I finished some shading on the sketch. I looked up as the screen door opened. Jesse was shirtless. He had his t-shirt thrown over his right shoulder and his tan skin was glistening from the sun hitting the thin layer of sweat that covered his body. I knew from the way his shirts clung to him that Jesse worked out, what I didn't know is that he was gorgeous. His pecs were clearly defined. He didn't have a six-pack, he had an eight-pack, and every muscle in his arm was toned. I bit my lower lip to contain an audible moan.

"My clothes are gross; I'm going to throw everything in the washer before I get in the shower." He kicked his shoes off by the door before walking in. I sat for a minute and then got up and followed him into the house. He had stripped to just his boxer briefs and was walking from the laundry room to his bedroom when I entered the house. He heard the door shut before he entered his room and he turned to look at me. "You okay? I figured you'd sketch longer."

"I think we need to talk."

"Can I shower first?" I shook my head. He turned and held his hand out to me. I walked toward him. "What's up?"

I put my arms around his waist and looked up at him locking my eyes on his dark brown eyes. I spoke quietly. "I know we just decided yesterday that we wanted this to be more than the friendship we originally started with. You know that I've only been with Kyle and that it was a bad experience." He nodded. "I thought I was going to need time before I was ready, but the more I spend time with you, the more I want to be with you, and I don't know how to know when I'm ready."

He pulled me in close. "You just know. I promise. You'll know. I'll know too. We're not ready. We might both want to, but we aren't ready. In the meantime, we are going to spend a lot of time together and we are going to know a lot about each other which is going to make when we are ready that much better."

"Thanks for being patient."

"Not anything you need to thank me for. I'm enjoying slow with you." He pulled me in close and kissed me. "Now I'm going to go take a shower and then I'll be out."

Twenty minutes later, he joined me on the couch for a video game tournament. He was right when he said he was a video game nerd. He had all the old systems and newer systems. He had a ridiculous amount of games. We decided on a classic systems and games tournament and spent most of the afternoon playing *Super Mario Brothers* and *Sonic*. I could not believe that he had *Duck Hunt*.

"I told you I was a video game nerd. Wait until you dig through that bottom bin and see all the original *Atari* stuff I have."

"Such a nerd." I giggled when I said it. He grabbed me and pulled me to him.

"Now that you've kicked my ass at all three games, what would you like to do? We can make dinner here and watch movies or we can go out." He brushed my hair behind my ear as he spoke.

"I like here." I leaned forward and kissed him.

When he slowed us, he said, "I like here too. I would like to take you on a real date one night though."

"We're both off on Wednesday, right?"

He nodded. "I'm off since I worked yesterday."

"Me too since I'm not teaching classes in the city. Do you have plans?"

"I do now. I'm spending the entire day with you. What do you want to do Sweetheart?"

"Spend the day with you. You choose." I repositioned so I was on his lap and leaned against him.

He wrapped his arms around me. "I'll plan something. Next weekend starting Friday, my friend Joey will be home on leave from the Army. He gets home Friday and leaves the following Saturday. We'll have a lot going on with him and most of the time everything will happen at Marco's because it's easier with Gabby."

"I should be back in my place by then, so it's fine. I can see you when he leaves."

He leaned forward and lowered his voice. "Not what I meant. I want you there with me. I meant I was letting you know so you could prepare to be around new people. Friday night will probably be a bigger party with 30 to 40 people. After that it will be us, Joey, his friend who is coming home with him, Shauna, Marco, Jenna, and Gabby. Mom will be around for at least part of the time. I want you there for as much of it as you want to be there for."

"Okay. I have plans with Brie that Friday, so I'll have to skip that, but other than work, I don't have anything else planned, so let me know what you want me around for, and I'll be there."

He pulled me to him and curled his arm around me. "I want you there for all of it."

"I can be there for all of it Jesse." I leaned forward and kissed him sweetly.

"Movie or series?" He brought up Netflix and started scrolling.

"Let's pick a series and when we don't know what to watch we can pick up where we left off."

"Love that idea. You pick. Nothing super girlie like *Gilmore Girls* or *Gossip Girl*. Other than that, I'm open to anything."

I scrolled through. "Do you like crime shows?"

"They're my favorite."

"Mine too. Original *NCIS*?"

He repositioned us on the couch, so we were laying down. He was against the back of the couch and had pulled me into him where my back was pressed against his chest and I was using his arm as a pillow. He had one arm over my hip. "Perfect. I watched that but not from the beginning and I never caught them consistently."

"Same." Three episodes later, I realized we never decided on dinner. "What do you want for dinner Jesse?"

"Anything easy."

"Let's make pizza dough and make pizza. We still have the salad."

"Sounds perfect."

We ate dinner on the couch while we watched a couple more episodes. Jesse washed the dishes and cleaned the kitchen after dinner. "Dishes are done, and the kitchen is clean. I would love to stay up late again tonight, but I open the garage tomorrow at six, so I need to leave at five-thirty. I need to head to bed. Do you need anything before I go crash?" I thought about it for a moment. I started to talk but stopped myself. He came over and stood behind the couch. "I'm an open book, remember? Just say it."

I moved onto my knees and leaned over the back of the couch to where he was standing. "Where do you want me to sleep tonight?"

"I want you to sleep wherever you are most comfortable. I'm hoping you want to sleep where you slept last night." He gently kissed me.

"That's what I was hoping because that's where I want to sleep. Let's go to bed."

Chapter 7

Jesse

The garage is always busy, but today felt busier than usual. I was able to get everything on Lexie's car done though, so I feel better about that.

"So what Saturdays are you working for me?" Marco asked as we locked up the front of the shop and made our way to the back exit.

I shook my head. "Still not a relationship, Marco. We're seeing what happens."

"You can change the title, but it's still a relationship. That's not a bad thing man. Just be sure it's what you want."

I stopped halfway between to the back door and turned and looked at him. "The only thing I know for sure is I've never experienced something like this, and I don't want her to leave my house."

"You're done. It's a relationship. Go get her a set of keys made."

I walked the rest of the way to the back exit and armed the building. Once it was armed and we exited, I locked the three locks before turning to look at Marco again. "She already has a set. She doesn't know that they're hers to keep as long as she wants them." He finished arming the garage and we parted ways.

I saw her in the studio space when I pulled into the driveway. *I like coming home to her. Shit. I'm so screwed. I don't want her to leave, but what if she doesn't want to stay? What if I'm only a distraction from what she went through with Kyle?*

"Hi, how was your day?" She called out to me as I walked across the yard to the back patio.

"We were busy. I got your car done. Tune-up, oil change, and brakes. You really needed brakes Sweetheart."

She shrugged her shoulders and made that cute face where she bites her lower lip, and her eyes get wide. "I'm not the best about car maintenance. I go by the sticker reminders and when lights come on."

I shook my head. "Telling a mechanic and car lover something like that is like punching me in the gut. How was your day?" I opened the screen door and stopped to check out the crab apple tree piece she had updated.

"Relaxing. I taught morning classes, so I was done at eleven. I saw Gabby. She was in my acrylic class. She asked if I was your girlfriend."

"What did you tell her?" I turned and looked at her across the patio.

"That we were new and still getting to know each other." She shrugged. "I don't know what we are."

I crossed the studio space and knelt in front of her. "I need to tell you something. I don't know what we are either. I told you that I'm not a relationship guy and then when we decided to be more than friends, I told you I didn't know how to be in a relationship. You asked me to keep doing what I was doing and promise my hands and lips were only on you." She nodded. "What you don't know is that I'm constantly battling an internal dialogue. I have never invited a woman back to my home. Ever. Now that I have and I know it's only until we know your place is safe, I don't want you to leave. I've never experienced this before. I can't stop thinking about you. I've never spent hours kissing someone. I've never enjoyed getting to know someone as I have with you. I have fun with you, Lexie. I enjoy everything about us. And I sure as hell have never used the words "us" and "we" when talking about a girl before. I'm pretty sure all of that means I want a relationship and I want you to be my girlfriend, but I also know you just got out of something that was truly messed up and you are stuck without options of safe places to be right now. I don't want you to choose me because you don't have any other option."

She leaned into me and placed her forehead on mine like I often do with her. She lowered her voice to just over a whisper, the volume that sends a jolt through me. "I choose you because you treat me well and because I've never experienced anything like this either. I still need us to go slow, but I choose you Jesse because I want you, not because I feel like I have to."

I leaned forward and kissed her deeply. When I slowed us, we were both breathless. "I need to tell you one more thing. The keys I gave you yesterday are yours to keep as long as you want them."

"I guess the next time Gabby asks, I can say I'm your girlfriend."

"Thank goodness." I captured her lips again. I started it as a gentle kiss and deepened it. I pulled her close to me and she parted her lips allowing me in. I massaged her tongue with mine and she let out of soft moan as I increased the pressure of my tongue on hers. She ran her fingers up and down my neck and across my shoulders. The oven timer brought us back to reality. "What's that?"

"Dinner. Go wash up and meet me at the table."

She had finished putting dinner on the table when I came in the room after changing. "This smells amazing."

"I made balsamic glazed salmon with roasted veggies." I put my arms around her waist and pulled her to me and placed four kisses down her neck.

"Thank you for making dinner. I appreciate it."

"You're welcome. I made extra so you have lunch tomorrow too."

I still had my arms wrapped around her waist, I pulled her closer to me and placed kisses down each side of her neck. "Thank you. The guys were pretty jealous of the eggplant parm I had today. I told them that not only are you smart, artistically talented, sweet, and funny, you're the best cook I've ever known and that's huge because Mom and Jenna can cook." I released her from my arms and held her chair out for her before sitting down. We talked for an hour about everything and nothing at all during dinner. "I'm going to need to up my workouts with you cooking for me Sweetheart." I set my napkin down next to my empty plate.

"Maybe I shouldn't tell you about dessert." She stood and started clearing dishes.

I stood up. "Stop. I clear and clean. But I do need to know more about dessert." I took the dishes and pan from her and started washing dishes.

"Well you ate all the brownies, so we needed something. I made chocolate lasagna."

"I don't know what that is, but I have a feeling it's going to be delicious."

She stood next to me at the sink and dried after I rinsed. "Chocolate cookie layer, topped with a cream cheese and whipped cream layer, topped with a chocolate pudding layer, topped with a layer of whipped cream topped with chocolate chips and chocolate shavings. Some people use Cool Whip, but I hate that stuff, so I made the whipped cream. To prevent us from eating the entire pan, I made it in individual serving cups and put some in containers you can take to work to share."

"How did I get so lucky to find you? Come here." I pulled her close to me and kissed her. I took two steps forward easing her back two steps, so she was pinned between me and the wall. She wrapped her arms over my shoulders, and I reached down and lifted her by her thighs and guided her legs to wrap around my waist. I supported her against the wall with my knee. Every whimper, murmur, and moan she made caused a reaction to jolt through my body. She ground against me. "Slow Baby. Still going slow." I knew we still needed to go slow, but there was part of me that was ready for more. She wasn't though and I wasn't going to push that. Everything at her pace.

"More." She softly whimpered.

"More what Sweetheart?"

"More everything."

I repositioned my hands so I could carry her to the couch. I dropped onto the couch gently and we continued to kiss. She repositioned to a straddling position and ground against me again. "Slow Baby."

"You said my pace, right?" I nodded. "Then we're good."

"We're not ready, not really. It's obvious we both want to, but let's take our time and enjoy getting there. It's always been a race to the finish line for me. You're different. You mean something to me, and I want this to mean something. I want to enjoy every moment of us getting there. Okay?"

"Okay."

We kissed some more and when we slowed, we were both breathless. I glanced toward the window and realized it was dark. Not dusk dark, but dark dark. I glanced at the clock on the wall. "That can't be, right? It's after ten. Did we kiss for two hours?"

She giggled in my arms. "I think we did."

"Bed. We need to go to bed."

"Shower. I need to shower. Then I can go to bed."

"That's my plan too. I usually shower as soon as I get home from work, but dinner was ready and I wanted to spend time with you, so I just changed. You can have the first shower if you want."

She stood up and started to walk toward my room. She lifted her tank top over her head. "Or we can share the shower." That was an invitation I was not going to decline. I followed her into my room.

"Are you sure?"

"Yes. We can still take things slow and share a shower and sleep in the same bed. We are taking things slow because we are enjoying every moment, right?"

"Right."

"Then let's enjoy this moment too." She took my hand and led me to the shower. She stripped completely and stepped into the water I had turned on. I pulled my shirt off and stepped out of my shorts. She pulled me into the shower. I slid my hands down her sides and rested them on her hips. She shyly said, "I've never done this before."

"Pretty sure you've showered before Babe."

"Not with someone."

I leaned down and kissed right below her ear. "Me either." I placed kisses along her shoulder and then returned my mouth to her neck. "Still not expecting anything. Let's share the shower and crawl in bed. I'll kiss you until we fall asleep. No pressure for anything else. I'm enjoying the view in this shower by the way. You are gorgeous." She turned bright red. "Sweetheart, if you've never been told that you're beautiful, they were blind. You are beautiful. Inside and out." I wrapped her in my arms and held her close to me.

"No one's ever said that to me before Jesse. I don't know how I'm supposed to respond to kind words."

"All you need to do is accept them and believe them." I placed a kiss on her forehead and rotated us. "You're hogging the water Babe, switch for a second. I let out a low moan as I watched her in the shower.

"What?"

"Sexy as hell Babe."

"What is?"

"Watching you."

"You're ridiculous and now you're the water hog. Switch so I can rinse." As we switched spots, I paused and pulled her close to me to steal kisses. She turned off the water when she was done and led me to the bedroom. I grabbed towels from the towel rack as we passed.

"What's going on in your head? I can see the wheels spinning." I sat at the end of the bed.

She stood in front of me. "I need you to know something." She paused. "I like being here and I am still here because I'm choosing to be. I don't feel like I'm forced to be here. I know that was a big thing for you in our discussions earlier. You needed to take things slow because you wanted me to have a choice. Well, I'm choosing to stay and I'm choosing to sleep in this room with you." She leaned down and kissed me.

I pulled her close. "I'm choosing you too. I've told you a few times that you mean something. This is all still new for me, but I need you to know that you mean something to me."

"I really like that Jesse. You're the only person who's ever said nice things to me and I'm not always sure how to respond."

"Open book. Tell me what you're thinking and what you're feeling and we're going to be fine. Now get your sexy ass in bed. We both need to sleep."

"I need pajamas. I need to go get them in the other room."

I threw her a t-shirt. "That dresser," I pointed to the one by the door, "is empty. You can move your stuff there if you want."

"I'll do it tomorrow when you're at work. I can throw the bedding from the guest room in the washer too. I don't plan on sleeping in there anymore."

"I like you in here." I crawled into bed and pulled her to me. "Sleep." She shook her head. "No?"

"Kiss. Then sleep. You promised to kiss until we fell asleep."

And we did. My alarm went off way too early. I woke up to Lexie using me as a pillow. I tried to slide out without waking her but was unsuccessful. "Sorry, Sweetheart. I have to get up, even though I'd rather stay here."

"Tomorrow. We get to sleep in tomorrow. I'll get up and make your coffee and breakfast while you get ready. I want to finish the painting I started yesterday with the same light, so I was going to get up with you." She got up and walked toward the door.

"Yes, tomorrow and I have a surprise planned. Thank you for making breakfast. I'll be out in a minute." I had to stop myself from saying something else. It was too soon. I couldn't yet. *Don't say it. You'll scare her away.* I pulled on my work pants and stepped into my boots. I had finished buttoning my shirt as I walked into the kitchen. "What is all of this?" I looked at the stack of containers on the counter.

"Salmon and veggies, salad, chocolate lasagna with enough to share. It's your lunch. I filled your thermos with coffee and just finished making egg and veggie scramble. What do you want to drink?" She set the plate at the counter and I sat on the barstool.

"Water please." I took a bite of breakfast and made the over the top moan that has become the routine. "So delicious. You're spoiling me."

"You work hard. You need good food." She set the water down and grabbed the spot next to me. As soon as I was finished, I leaned over and kissed her sweetly. "Thank you. I'll see you tonight. Call me if you need me."

"Have a nice day. Oh wait, what do you want for dinner?"

"Whatever's easy or we can go out," I called out as I walked to the back door.

"I like here."

"Me too. Have a good day." I stopped halfway down the back steps. *No, it's too soon.* I walked over to my bike and put the thermos and lunch she'd packed me in the saddlebag, put on my leather jacket and helmet, and backed out of the driveway.

I pulled back into the driveway almost 12 hours later. It had been a long day. We needed to expand and bring on a couple more employees. I looked over at the studio area and expected to find Lexie there, but she wasn't. Her car was parked in the driveway, so I knew she was home. I walked up the back steps and into the screened porch. I took my boots off before walking into the house. As soon as I opened the door, I heard her. She was in the kitchen singing. "I'm home," I called out as I opened the door.

"I know. I heard you. As soon as I heard your bike on the street, I came in from sketching to start the last part of dinner. I figured I'd time it so you could shower and change."

I walked over to her and pulled her in close and kissed her softly. "I missed you today."

"I missed you too."

"How long until dinner?"

"15 minutes."

"I only need 10, so I'm kissing you first." She turned toward me and pressed her body against me, and I kissed her deeply. I slowed us and pulled away from her. "I'll be back in less than 10 so I can help you."

I returned in seven minutes and found dinner on the table. "I gave us both glasses of water, do you want anything else?" She asked.

"Water is perfect. I thought when you asked me what I wanted for dinner tonight I said whatever's easy. This looks like another fancy meal."

"Fancy can be easy, plus I love to cook but it's always just me, so I don't get a chance to."

"I love that you love cooking for me. I appreciate it." I kissed her on the cheek and took the water glasses from her to take them to the table. "Go sit. I'll bring anything else out."

"Thank you. It's the waters and the salad from the fridge. Everything else is out."

I brought everything to the table. "What amazing meal did you make for us tonight?"

"I did a little research for this one." She reached her arm across the table and opened the lid on the pot. She turned to me and smiled.

"Pozole. Who told you?"

"Jenna."

"Thank you."

"You're welcome. You've been so good to me and done so much, I wanted to make your favorite meal. I called Jenna and she told me this is always your request when you get to pick a favorite and Marco's mom always makes it for your birthday."

"Hand me your bowl, I'll serve Sweetheart."

I sat down after I served pozole for both of us. She handed me the tortilla warmer. I pulled one out. "You made the tortillas?"

"Of course, I made them."

"Before I eat this entire thing of pozole and go into a food coma, I need to ask you something."

"You can ask me anything"

"Have you ever ridden on a motorcycle?"

"Dirt bike, but not a motorcycle."

"Do you want to? I was thinking it would be a perfect day for a ride tomorrow since we have the day off. It's twenty miles to the lake or we could plan something further if we wanted to make it a longer trip."

"I'd love to go on a ride. What I would like is if you planned the day completely. No one has ever planned something they thought I'd like. Just tell me what to wear and if I need to bring anything."

"You're not the only one who called Jenna today. I called to see if she was okay with you borrowing her helmet and stuff. She said she thought Marco still had it all and it was fine to borrow. She hasn't ridden since the accident. I have the helmet and leathers for you in case you said yes. I grabbed them from the house."

"Thank you. What time do you want to leave?"

"Nine. I'm going for the long ride and we want to get going before it's too hot. When you layer, put on something you can get wet in. Then something you'll want to wear when you aren't on the bike and finally long sleeves. You'll need to wear jeans when you're on the bike."

"I can do that. Thank you for planning."

"You're welcome. I think you're going to love it."

She smiled at me across the table. "It's a day with you. I'll love it."

We finished dinner and made our way to the couch to continue our Netflix binge. Usually the night before my day off, I'd be out, but this was so much better. I could get used to this. No, it was more than that. I wanted to get used to this. I already had gotten used to coming home to Lexie in the kitchen or on the porch studio. I liked her here.

Halfway through the second episode she looked up at me and asked, "do you want dessert?"

"Is that code for kissing?"

"I meant actual dessert, but kissing is better."

"Dinner was so amazing I can't even consider actual dessert, but I definitely want kissing. Can we move to the bed though? We both look like we are going to crash soon." She sat up and took my hand and led me to the bedroom. I caught up with her right before she got to the doorway and I lifted her as I held her against me. "Thank you again for dinner. And in case I haven't made it clear, I like having you here."

She turned and looked at me over her shoulder. "I like being here." I leaned down and kissed her softly. When we got to the foot of the bed, I picked her up a little higher and tossed her gently onto the bed. I crawled up on the bed. I turned so I was on my left side next to her. I traced up her leg from her knee to her hip with my right hand and she scooted closer. She reached her left hand out and placed it on the hem of my shirt and she started to tug it up. I reached over my shoulder and grabbed the neck of my shirt and pulled it up. She placed the palm of her hand on my abs and started tracing their outline with her fingers. I leaned down and kissed her. When my hand stopped on her hip, she quietly asked "why'd you stop?"

"Why'd I stop what?"

"Your hand."

"Still taking our time and going slow. Was there something you wanted?"

She nodded and took my hand and guided it to the waistband of her shorts. "Please. I need you. I can't stand it. Please."

"Are you sure?" She nodded. "I need words Sweetheart."

"Yes. I'm sure."

"As soon as you want me to stop, tell me. Tell me if anything doesn't feel good and I'll fix it."

"Okay."

I moved my hands to her waistband slowly slid down her shorts. "Lift up a little Sweetheart." She did and I pulled them the rest of the way off. I started tracing back up her leg. This time starting at her ankle. I worked my way to her knee and paused.

"Keep going." I traced up to her mid-thigh and stopped. "Stop stopping."

"Keep talking sweetheart. I need you to tell me what you want."

"You're doing this on purpose!"

"I am. I know you haven't had control before. I want you to understand that I am listening, and I will do what you want. Tell me to stop and I stop. Tell me to keep going and I keep going. Okay?"

"Okay. Keep going. Now!"

"I like you bossy Baby. Keep doing that." I worked my hand up the rest of her thigh to her hip and I quickly traced back down the leg.

"No! Where are you going?"

I laughed and took the other ankle in my hand and did the same slow trace up her leg. This time when I got the top of her thigh, she grabbed my wrist and guided me to the center. "Here, I want you here. Now. Please."

I leaned down and kissed her softly and my fingers moved the edge of her panties to the side. I traced her lips with my tongue, and she parted to let me in. While I massaged her tongue with mine, my finger traced up and down her slit. She took her hand and guided me where she wanted me, and I slowly slid a finger in. She arched up slightly and positioned where she needed me. She moaned "more" as my finger worked in and out. I added a second finger and increased the speed. She softly said "faster", and I complied. While I worked in and out, my thumb found her clit and I applied pressure to it in gentle circles. I felt her clench around my fingers and her hands dropped to her side and she gripped the blanket. She softly let out a moan.

She was breathless and whispered in my ear. "What's happening?"

"What's happening, Sweetheart?"

"I'm so hot everywhere. My heart is racing. Everything went white. It was like electricity throughout my body."

I whispered in her ear. "Orgasm." I kissed down her neck and my hands moved to her hips to slide her closer to me. "I'm assuming that was your first one."

"Well I thought I had them before, but I was wrong. So wrong. Nothing has ever felt like that."

"I like that I was your first orgasm." I kissed her softly and guided us both toward the top of the bed and placed us on the pillows without breaking the kiss. "Sleep Sweetheart. It's late." I threw the top cover over us.

"What about you? This did nothing for you." She started to reach for me.

I shook my head and placed my hand on top of hers to stop her. "That was amazing. Watching you, hearing you make those noises, and feeling you clench around my fingers. That was amazing Sweetheart. Let's sleep. I don't need anything else tonight."

"Are you sure?"

"As sure as I am that I like having you here and that you mean something. All of this means something." I repositioned us so her head was on my chest and I could wrap my arms around her.

"What does it mean Jesse?" She looked up at me.

"Something that I feel like it's too early to say and that if I say it, it will scare you away."

"If it's three words, I've been thinking it too and scared to say it for the same reason."

I slowly took a breath in and let it out. I looked deep into her beautiful gray-blue eyes and said words I never thought I'd say. "I love you, Lexie."

"I love you too, Jesse."

I pulled her in closer to me. "I've never said that before."

"I've never meant it before. I said it, but only because he made me. It never meant anything other than an out from being hurt."

"I hate that these words have that memory for you. I'm going to do everything I can to try to erase that." I ran my fingers through her hair.

She rotated in my arms, so she was completely pressed against me. "It's already working. The more I hear kind things from you, the more I believe them. Thank you for loving me and showing me what love should be Jesse."

"You're welcome, Sweetheart. Thank you for letting me figure all this out. I was so set in the 'I don't do relationships' mindset, I never figured out how a relationship is supposed to be."

"You're already the best boyfriend. You listen. You pay attention to things. You spend time with me. You make me a priority. You make me feel loved. Even before you said the words, I knew you loved me." She kissed down the side of my neck and traced her fingers across my abs.

"You make it easy Lexie. It's like I can't not spend time with you. I think about you all day at work. I love coming home to you. I love falling asleep with you each night and waking up with you in the morning. I don't want to be anywhere on my time off other than with you. Everything that I was scared of that kept me from trying relationships before is easy with you."

"I love all of that too Jesse."

"Stay."

"Stay? Stay where?"

"Here."

She smiled the smile that lights up my world. "I am staying here. You wanted me to stay the week until we knew he was staying away."

"Stay longer."

"How much longer?"

"Forever."

"What are you asking me, Jesse?"

"Move in. Bring the rest of your stuff. Fill the house with your stuff. You're what's been missing to make it a home. Stay. Forever."

"Are you sure?"

I nodded. "As sure as I am that I love you. Will you stay?"

"Yes. We can bring some more of my stuff. I can't give up my place yet. I won't stay there, but I can't give it up yet."

"Whenever you're ready. And in case it's not clear, I'm still enjoying slow. No pressure."

"Not yet, but soon. I know it will be soon. I love you, Jesse."

"I love you, Lexie."

Chapter 8

Lexie

I pulled my helmet off after Jesse took off his. "That was amazing. I was so scared at first, but that was so amazing. I did what you told me to and held on to you every time I got scared."

Jesse reached around and grabbed me, pulling me forward to him. "You did so good Sweetheart. This was a long ride, and you did everything I told you to. I'm so glad you liked it." He kissed me deeply. "I love you."

"I love you too." I was never going to get tired of hearing those words or saying them. "Where are we?" We were parked in front of a small store that had a restaurant sign on one in and a post office sign on the other. The stairs in the middle lead to green wooden double doors and had the word market written above them. There was one car in the six spot parking area.

"We are at one of my favorite places in the world. This is the town my mom's parents grew up in. If you can believe it, it's smaller than Woods Lake."

"Nowhere is smaller than Woods Lake Jesse."

"This town is. The highway divides it in half, three blocks on each side and it's five blocks long. This little market is also a restaurant, the post office, and there's a two-bedroom apartment above it where my Grandma grew up. My mom's sister still lives there, and she owns this place. We're going to grab the very best sandwiches in the world and finish our day with a ride out to picnic in the hills on private property my family still owns. I need to get the gate key from my aunt." He took my hand and led me into the market.

As soon as we were in the door, I heard a voice call out. "Jesse. I'm so glad you're here. I was so excited to get your voicemail. The key's in the normal spot." Then I saw her. The family resemblance was strong. She had dark brown hair and the same dark brown eyes that are so dark they almost match the pupils. "You must be Lexie. I'm Maria." She grabbed me in a hug. "You must be important. He's never brought anyone home to visit."

"She means something. I never thought I'd say that about anyone." He said as he came from the back room with a set of keys. "Thank you for this. We will bring them back on our way out of town."

"Oh no. No, you don't mister. You don't get to just stop by, pick up lunch, go to the property, and then drop off keys. What are your plans for dinner?"

"Take out and a movie at home." He answered as he handed me a deli menu.

"Nope. When you're done on the property, come back here and I'll make dinner for all of us. The restaurant opens officially at five, but I'll cook early if you're back early. That way you can get back down the hills before it's too dark."

"We'd love to." I jumped in and answered. Jesse wrapped his arm around my waist.

"Great, now what do you want for lunch. Jesse said 'a couple of sandwiches' but no details. I'll make whatever you want, take a look at the deli menu."

"Jesse, what are you getting?"

They both replied at the same time "BBQ tri-tip with the works, extra sauce, and horseradish."

I giggled. I looked at the sandwich menu, there were so many choices. Jesse leaned over. "Everything is amazing. You can't go wrong."

"Italian grilled cheese without the pickles or caramelized onions please."

"Good choice. It's so good." Jesse wrapped his arms around my waist and pulled me close to him.

"It's pepperoni, prosciutto, mozzarella, and provolone on asiago bread. How can it not be?"

"Two sandwiches and what else? Any sides? I made antipasto salad and the tortellini pasta salad you love Jesse."

"Yes, definitely to both of those. Go pick a drink Sweetheart and I'll grab waters. Can we get some of the fruit salad too and can I be obnoxious and not get the honeydew? Lexie doesn't like it."

"No problem. I wouldn't do it for you, but she can have whatever she wants." Marie winked at him as she said it.

He stood at the deli counter and talked to Maria while I grabbed my drink.

"Do you want anything Jesse?" I asked from the drink area.

"Peach tea, please. Thank you."

Jesse paid for lunch even though Maria told him not to worry about it and we said goodbye. We loaded the food and drinks into the saddlebags and headed to the property. He turned from the paved street to a wide dirt road, then onto a small dirt road that slowly narrowed. We reached a locked gate and Jesse stopped and unlocked it. Once we were through it, he locked it again and headed about 15 minutes into the property. There was a huge oak tree with a wooden picnic table and the most beautiful view I've ever seen. We were surrounded by mountains and ranch land as far as we could see. There was no one else for miles.

"Wow. This is beautiful."

"It's my favorite place in the world. I'm glad you like it. Are you hungry for lunch now, or can I show you something first?"

"Show me something."

"Go ahead and take off the layers, we're here until whenever we decide to leave. I even remembered to grab other shoes for you." He opened the saddlebag and handed me my slip-on tennis shoes. "We can leave everything at the table. No one else will be out today. We have all 50 acres to ourselves."

"In case I forget to tell you tonight, thank you for today. It's already been the best day ever Jesse." He kissed me gently.

"You're welcome Sweetheart and I think it's about to get better, come on." He took my hand and led me down a path. We walked for about 10 minutes and then I saw it.

"No way! I was expecting a lake or creek or something. Not this. There's a hot spring on the property?" He shook his head and held up seven fingers. "Seven?"

"Yep. There's seven. This means you're going to have to come here at least six more times so you can try them all. We are starting with my favorite."

"Why is it your favorite?"

"Because it's right in the middle temperature-wise a couple of others are super-hot. It's deep enough to soak in, plus it fits two." He set our towel on the large rock near the springs, kicked off his shoes, and took his shirt off. He slid off his jeans and stepped into the springs wearing only his boxer briefs. "Your turn."

I slid my cotton shorts off and pulled my tank top off. Leaving a light blue lace bra and matching bottoms. "I didn't bring my suit to your house since I didn't think I'd need one."

"You can stay in all that lace or" he paused and give me the eye wiggle that sends butterflies through me.

"Or what?"

"It's 50 acres and we are completely alone. You can take it off. Might be more comfortable on the ride home. It's up to you." I slowly removed all the lace setting it on the rock next to us. Jesse held out his hand to me and helped me step into the hot springs. "You continue to surprise me, Sweetheart."

"How so?"

"The first night at the bar when we were playing catch up, you described yourself as shy. You're never shy with me."

"Because you've shown me that I can trust you."

"Completely Baby. You can trust me completely." He sat in the springs and pulled me to him. "Come sit with me." He pulled me to his lap and wrapped me in his arms. I leaned back so my head was resting on the space between his neck and right shoulder.

"I love it here. Thank you for bringing me."

"You're welcome. I'm glad you love it here. It's a quiet getaway and doesn't take too long to get to, but long enough that it seems far." He wrapped his arms around me tighter and rested his chin on my shoulder.

"It's perfect."

"Tell me something you've never told anyone." He kissed the side of my neck after making the request.

"I feel like you already know everything about me, Jesse. My mom walked when I was three. By the time I was eight, Brie was basically raising us, and we moved out at fourteen and sixteen. We didn't see much of my dad after that. He died three years later."

He pulled me in closer and draped a leg over mine when I talked about my dad. He lowered his voice. "I knew he wasn't around. I didn't know he died. I'm so sorry Sweetheart. You were too young to go through that even if he wasn't around much, if at all. Want to tell me about it or change the subject?"

I turned and looked at him over my shoulder. "I'll talk about it." I rested my head against him again. "Do you remember that drunk driving accident about five years ago? It was the truck that crossed the line and hit the car with the teenagers in it and everyone died."

He took a deep breath in and let it out. "I do. It was between Woods Lake and Badger out on the old highway. That was your dad?"

"Yes. He had two other people in the truck with him and four teenagers were in the car he hit. We didn't have much as it was. Brie and I had been out of the house for years at that point, but what was left, was lost in lawsuits. We didn't attempt to fight anything because we knew we couldn't win. They went after all his assets which was the house, life insurance, retirement, and bank accounts. They got it all and split it between the six families. The house was the hardest because it was the house my grandpa had grown up in."

He turned me to face him and wiped the tears from my eyes. "I'm so sorry Sweetheart." He held me while I cried and didn't say anything else. He just held me. After about twenty minutes, I told him what it was like for me when Brie got married at seventeen and divorced a year later starting the short marriage and divorce cycle. "I was only fifteen when she got married the first time, but I ended up with rent on my own while still in high school. It was hard Jesse. At that point, I was basically on my own. Thankfully, the owner of the building we were in at the time was a sweet older lady and she knew that we were on our own. She told me to keep paying what I could and not worry about full rent. As soon as a smaller place was open, she had me move in there. Not because of the rent, but for utilities to be less. When she passed, her son sold the building and I moved where I am now. When I graduated from high school, I got a full scholarship for a two-year art program in the city. I talked to admissions and they worked with me to do an accelerated fifteen-month program so that the scholarship could pay for housing. I kept my studio here because the rent is cheap, and I'm locked into what I was paying when I first moved in. I didn't want to lose that, plus it gave Brie a place to be when her marriage ended. Her second marriage was a disaster and ended pretty quickly too. I think she believes if she doesn't say yes and get married that they'll leave, and she'll end up alone. We both grew up in the same situation, but she feels more abandoned because she ended up being the one to take care of me and had no one to take care of her. Where I want to make sure whoever I end up with is my one and done, she wants to be married because she believes it's how she's guaranteed someone to take care of her. I guess that's why even though I get frustrated by her, I can't give up on her."

"I guess that makes sense. She ended up a parent at age ten and never had anyone to take care of her and now she's looking for that. Where you and I had someone or in my case multiple someones to take care of us. You've known you want the picket fence, ring, and kids and I've avoided it because I don't know what a healthy relationship truly is or if I'm capable of it."

I looked at him. "You're capable of it. You're already doing it. We're new, but since the first night we hung out at Rocky's before you covered the bar, you've always put me first and we were just talking that night. Everything you've done to make sure I'm safe, take care of my car, replace my apartment door, and make me a priority shows that you know how to be a part of a healthy relationship. You might not know it, but it's all anyone wants Jesse. We want someone to make us feel important and to take care of us."

He leaned forward and turned my head slightly before kissing me gently. "Thank you for telling me all of that, not just about me, but about your hard stories."

"You're welcome, Jesse. I think that sharing hard stories is what will make us stronger because we already know we love each other for the fun, easy, and silly stuff, but loving the hard is what means we can make it through anything."

"You already know most of my hard. My parents and bouncing from place to place. The other hard is Ricky. It's what destroyed all of us: me, Marco, Joey, Jenna, especially Jenna and partially Shauna and Tony. They weren't there that night. Shauna was visiting her Grandma and usually wasn't able to go out to races anyway unless Joey snuck her out of the house. Tony was too young. He was only fourteen when it happened. It was a night that destroyed us all but created the us we are now." I turned and wrapped my arms around his waist and leaned into him while he told the story. "It was the second to last race of the night. We didn't do call-outs or any of that stuff. Numbers went into a bag, whoever's number matched yours is who you raced. I had already raced. Jenna had just finished, and Marco was in the last race. Joey and Ricky had pulled the same number, so they were racing each other. We didn't do that pussy eighth of a mile bullshit. A street race is a quarter-mile. No NOS or any of that all crap. Straight racing based on who had the better faster car. We don't know what happened." His voice slowed and lowered while he shared. "Ricky's car literally exploded and engulfed in flames about halfway through the race. Something, we still don't know what, flew off of his or out of his and hit Joey causing him to spin and flip into the tree." His eyes filled with tears. He took a deep breath and let it out before continuing. "There was nothing we could do to get Ricky out. I helped get Joey out before his car caught fire. Marco grabbed Jenna and wrapped her in his arms and pulled her onto the ground and pinned her down so she couldn't try to get to Ricky. She still doesn't remember anything after seeing the explosion and until waking up at Mom's house. She's been in therapy for almost ten years working through all her family stuff and Ricky's death. She moved out of her dad's house two days after the accident and Mom did whatever needed to be done so she could stay there permanently."

I leaned forward and kissed him quickly. "Jesse, that sounds so awful. I get losing someone in an accident, but I didn't have to watch it happen." He pulled me close and pressed my chest into his. "Thank you for telling me."

"You're welcome, Sweetheart. That's my hardest story. Is your dad's yours?"

I shook my head. "The abuse from Kyle is the hardest, but I think you understand all of that."

He nodded. "I do. I don't need you to tell me details Sweetheart, but when you are ready or if you are ready, I'll listen."

"I was nineteen when I met him, and he was so different from anyone I had known. He was generous with his money and took me out to expensive dinners and fancy places. He bought me fancy clothes to wear. I thought someone taking care of you by buying you things meant they loved you. The only way I'd ever seen love is through gifts, so it's all I knew.

I learned quickly it doesn't. I was naïve and the first time he hit me, I stayed because he apologized. The next time I stayed because he said it was an accident and I believed him. Six months in, it had become normal. It was always followed by apologies and gifts. Things would be good for a month or two and it would cycle again. I broke up with him and he left for about a month and he showed up apologizing and asking for another chance. Things were good for about four months and then he started going into fits of rage over little things. I tried to end things, but he broke my door down, the first time. The time I already told you about was the third time." I took a deep breath in and let it out. Jesse wiped the tears from my eyes. "He knew that I had never been with anyone and at first he was patient about it and then he wasn't anymore. He made me feel guilty for not being ready and when I finally said yes, it was so rough and hurt so much I didn't want to anymore, but that just made him aggressive." I paused.

Jesse kissed me softly. "You can keep going if you want to or you can stop. All at your speed." He pulled me in close to him. "I love that you trust me enough to tell me about all of this, but I can see that it's really hard for you. Baby steps Sweetheart, just tell me what you can."

"I want to tell you. I asked once, just once, why we only hung out in the city or in Woods Lake and we never went to his place. He threw me into the wall for pestering him and not trusting him. That was why I ended things six months ago. I had been hit, kicked, and punched on and off for almost three years. I was done. When he kicked my door in the last time, I was home and he fought dirty. I ended up pretty bruised and swollen. When I opened the door the day you came over to swim, I didn't check the peephole because I thought it was you. I was so scared Jesse. First, because I didn't think I could survive another fight and second, because I didn't want you to walk in on it and see it happen or end up involved." I repositioned so I was straddled across him and I placed my forehead on his. I lowered my voice. "I was so incredibly thankful when you walked in the door because, in the few hours, we had spent together the night before, I knew you'd never be like him."

He shook his head. "Never. I'm your safe place for always Sweetheart. You're safe with me."

"I know. You've shown me that since the very beginning. I know I never have to worry about not being safe again."

"Never." He leaned forward and kissed me sweetly. I took our sweet gentle kiss and deepened it. He pulled back and slowed us. "I love you, Lexie."

"I love you, Jesse. Let's go picnic and share some not hard stories before we go hang out with Maria." We got out of the hot spring and he wrapped me in the towel. Once I was dressed in my shorts and tank, he took my hand and led me back to the picnic table.

He told me about Ricky's dream for all of them to run a garage together and how Marco was the first to be able to start a shop and the plans to buy in and help it grow. I told him about my dream to open a kid space art studio that could offer classes like I offer through the community center but would also have creative centers for parents to bring their kids to have access to materials and explore. By the time he was done sharing stories, I already felt more comfortable about our upcoming week with the group while Joey was home.

At dinner, Maria told me every hilarious baby Jesse story she could remember. She told the sweet stories of Jesse helping older neighbors and family friends with yard work and small repairs even from a young age. She hugged me when we left. "I'm glad you came and stayed for dinner. I think I'll be seeing a lot of you."

I hugged her back. "I hope so. I'm not planning on going anywhere."

"Good. You're good for him and he's a good man. He needs time, but he'll get there." She winked at me before handing Jesse some of his favorite salads from the deli.

I left feeling like I knew everything about Jesse. I had never felt that connected to someone before. No one had ever known me the way he does because no one had taken the time to get to know me. *I'm ready. We're ready.* I know he's been ready but has been waiting for me.

As soon as we were off the bike in the driveway and out of our helmets, we took off all the layers, and I kissed him harder, deeper, and longer than I had before. I reached for his belt and said, "I'm ready."

chapter 9

Jesse

She reached for my waistband. "I'm ready. Now. I'm ready now." She started unfastening my belt. I placed my hand on top of hers stopping her.

"Are you sure?"

"Now. I'm 100% sure. I've been sure for a few days, but I wanted to be extra sure. Please. I can't wait any longer. I need you now."

I led her into the house and to the couch. I pulled her onto my lap. "Serious talk first. I get my annual screening. I had it two months ago. I haven't been with anyone in almost four months. I've never not used a condom."

"I've only been with Kyle. I haven't been with him in over six months and as soon as I knew he had a side girl, I got tested and got a six-month follow-up test. We always used condoms and I'm on the pill."

He kissed me. "Tell me what you like and what you don't."

"I like everything we've done. Nothing before ever made me feel like that. Everything with him was so fast and hurt always."

"Slow and sweet Baby. We are starting slow and sweet. I'm going to make up for everything before. It should never hurt in a bad way. You tell me if anything doesn't feel good and I'll fix it."

She leaned forward and kissed me. She was taking charge tonight and I liked that. I knew she needed that. Sex had never been on her terms before and there was one thing that I was going to make sure of first. I slid my hand down her side to her waistband down the front of her shorts. "I'm good. I'm ready. You don't need to."

I shook my head. "Ladies first, always, for everything Sweetheart. It will feel better if you are really ready." I slid my hand further down and placed my other hand on her hip. "You're still in charge of the kissing, I'm going to guide you with my hand on your hip while I take care of you. Everything tonight is about giving you a great experience."

"I love you." She whispered as she kissed me.

"I love you too. Tell me if anything doesn't feel good. I'll fix it."

She nodded. I slid my fingers to the edge of her panties and pushed them to the side. She had quickened her movement. "Slow Baby." She took my lips with hers and nibbled on my bottom lip and traced my lip with her tongue, I parted and let her in. When she increased the pressure on my tongue, I slid two fingers in her and guided her hip movements. She moaned. I applied pressure to her clit while guiding her rocking movements. She moaned again. She was right. She was ready, but taking this time would help later plus ladies first, always. I slid my fingers further up her wall and massaged the G as I added more pressure to the clit. She clenched around me threw her head back and called out my name. She collapsed forward onto my shoulder. I slid my fingers out and gently removed my hand from her shorts. "Good Baby?"

"So good." She placed her head on my shoulder and wrapped her arms around my neck as I scooped her up and carried her to bed.

I kicked off my shoes when I entered the room. I set her on the center of my bed before sliding onto the bed next to her. "Besides slow and sweet, do you have any requests Sweetheart?" I kissed her neck.

She paused and thought. "Music because silence makes my mind spin. I can't turn off the constant internal thoughts." I reached for my phone and set it on the sexy playlist before turning off the ringtone and message alerts, so we weren't interrupted. I put it in the speaker dock and hit play. "If I think of anything else, I'll let you know." I turned the speaker on and began slowly kissing her sweetly. I ran my hands down her sides and rested them on her hips. The song changed and *Pony* came on. She burst into giggles. "I have a request Jesse, strip."

"Baby, you are welcome to strip for me."

She shook her head. "Not me, you. Plus, I've already been completely naked for you today. It's your turn."

"You want the full Channing Tatum *Magic Mike* dance, don't you?"

"Hell yeah. If you're offering."

I reached over and set the song to restart and hit pause. "When I tell you to, hit play." I got up and walked over to my dresser. I grabbed a couple of things from the drawers and walked into the bathroom to change.

"What's taking you so long?" She called out from the bedroom.

"You said you want the full effect. I need to change." If she wanted the full effect, I was giving it to her. I pulled on my white tank top, put on my zip-up hoodie sweatshirt, pulled on the black athletic pants, and the red baseball hat. "Hit play sweetheart." I put the hoodie on over the hat and waited until the song came on and did my best Channing impression and walked on "stage" meaning into the bedroom. Once she could see me, I took the hoodie off, unzipped the sweatshirt, and let it fall. She had the biggest smile on her face making this ridiculous silliness worth it. I did my best Channing moves with the side to side slide and pelvic thrust with the upper body roll. I worked my way lower and dropped to the ground. At which point she dove from her spot in the middle of the bed to a laying position across the bed so she could hang off the bed to see me as I did the floor moves. When I popped back up to my feet, I told her "the next time I drop, I'm dropping over you on that bed." She scooted to the middle of the bed. I worked my way to the bed before I pulled my tank top off. Once I removed it, I dropped onto the bed over her. By this point, she was in a fit of giggles and I captured her lips with mine.

"Best strip ever. You were better than the movie Jesse."

"Liar, but I'm glad you liked it." She reached for my waistband and gently tugged. I slid out of my pants and pulled her closer to me.

"It was the best because it was for me and it took all my nervousness away and reminded me that it's us and we always have fun together, so I don't need to be nervous because this is going to be good."

"It's going to be great because it's us and you don't need to be nervous. Sex is fun Sweetheart. It should always be fun. I will Channing Tatum style strip for you every day if you need me to." I leaned forward and kissed her sweetly.

"I love you, Jesse."

"I love you too, Lexie."

"Thank you for waiting for me to be ready."

"It's not anything you need to thank me for. You're worth it. We are worth it. Now, do you need anything else from me before we continue?"

"A different song, please. I can watch you strip to *Pony* and I can silly make out to it, but I need something else."

"Something slow and sweet to keep the mind spin away. I know exactly the one. It's perfect for us." I grabbed my phone and pulled up my music app and downloaded *Wild Love* by James Bay. "This is the song that describes how I feel about us, Sweetheart." I set it to repeat.

"Perfect." She reached up to me and guided me down to her by placing her hand on my cheek. I took her lips with mine and gently kissed her. She let out of a soft moan. The moan instantly sent a message through my body and I feel myself harden. "Okay, Sweetheart, talk to me. You should always come first, what do you want?" I was tracing my fingers up the inside of her thigh.

"You, soft and sweet. You've given me everything else already before we moved to the bed, I'm ready for you. I need you. But I do have a request."

"Anything."

"I want to straddle across you and wrap my legs around your waist so you can hold me close to you. I need to feel you everywhere."

I moved so I could prop against the headboard and support us. I grabbed a condom from my nightstand drawer while I moved and reached out for her. "Come here, Sweetheart." I protected us and then when she was by my side, I grabbed the bottom of her top and pulled it up and over her head. I dropped it on the floor. I guided her across my lap and down. Stopping halfway so she could adjust before she took me in completely. "Wrap your legs, Baby." She did and I adjusted our position slightly. "Are you good?"

"So good." She began rocking us. I loved seeing her take control of us. In past weeks together she found her voice. There's nothing sexier than a woman who is confident about what she wants in her sex life and Lexie had become very confident. She was still quiet around others, but at home when we were kissing, and in bed, she was vocal. I loved it. "Jesse, harder. I need you harder." I bucked up a little faster and harder. She wrapped her arms around my shoulders and pressed her body against me. "Yes, Yes. I love feeling you everywhere against me and in me." She put her forehead against mine and looked me deep in my eyes. This was so different for me. I was used to be the one in complete control and never eye contact because no one before her had mattered. I was loving this with her because it was new, and it meant something. For the first time, it meant something. She bit her lower lip and slowed her motions slightly.

I leaned forward and whispered. "Stuck?" She nodded. "Just tell me, Baby. I'll get you there." I took her mouth with mine and she parted her lips. I glided my tongue in and massaged her tongue with mine. I kept one hand on the small of her back and slid the other one around her side and down her stomach. She realized what I was doing and nodded her head. I worked toward her center and while she rocked and I matched her speed as I bucked up into her, I worked her clit with two fingers. I felt her clench around me, and her forehead dropped to my shoulder. I continued to work her clit while I bucked into her faster and harder, bringing us both over the edge. "Oh my God, Jesse. That was amazing. I'm so glad we waited because I know I needed to, but I sort of wish we were doing this from the first day we hung out because nothing has ever been this great."

"It was this great because we didn't rush and I'm so glad we waited Sweetheart because this was the first time it's ever meant something. You mean something. I love you, Lexie." I wrapped my arms around her and pulled her into my chest.

"I love you too, Jesse. I'm glad we were each other's first mean something." She rested her head on my shoulder and wrapped her arms around me.

"Me too. Let me up for a second. I'm going to take care of this, and I'll be right back." I returned to our bed and found her curled on her side in the middle of the bed. I slid in bed behind her and curled up around her. "Sleep sweetheart. It's been a long day. I love you."

"I love you too. Thank you for the best day ever."

"You're welcome. I don't have to be at work until nine tomorrow. You sleep and I'll take breakfast duty." I pulled her close to me and pulled the blanket over us and we were both asleep within minutes.

Chapter 10

Lexie

I woke a little after six. My body had adjusted to the early mornings and I couldn't sleep anymore, but I wasn't getting out of bed. Jesse's arms were wrapped around me and I could hear him breathing slow, deep breaths while he was sound asleep. Yesterday was amazing. I thought we were going for a ride on the motorcycle and having lunch. I didn't expect to meet his aunt and visit his family's property. Jesse may have never committed and been in a relationship before, but he had to me right from the start. I knew the rumors and the talk, but I knew that things with us were different. He made sure I was safe and always put me first. This was new and was going to take time to accept because it was the first time someone had done these things and expected nothing in return.

I felt Jesse start to stir so I scooted my butt over toward him rubbed against him. He held me tighter. "Good morning Sweetheart. How long have you been up?"

"About half an hour."

He kissed down the side of my neck. "You could have woken me."

"I was enjoying being wrapped in your arms."

He pulled me in closer. "This has quickly become my favorite way to sleep."

"Mine too." I reached back and put my hand on his hip. "Do you teach today?"

"Nope. I'm here today. I'm going to finish the crab apple tree and then the sketch."

"I love the tree painting so far. We'll have to decide where we want it. When do I get to see the sketch?"

"It's a piece for the summer festival show so at the show."

"I can't convince you to let me see it early?" He kissed right in that spot on my neck that drives me wild. He discovered it early on and used it against me regularly.

"No. You'll see others, but this is the one I want to save. I'm pretty sure it's going to be the piece I put in the auction."

"If you're sure I can't change your mind, let's talk breakfast. I can make two things. Pancakes and fancy pancakes. Which would you like?"

"What are fancy pancakes?"

"Pancakes with chocolate chips or sprinkles or both?"

"Fancy pancakes please." He kissed me sweetly before getting out of bed. He pulled on basketball shorts as he walked out of the room.

I rolled out of bed and headed for the shower. I heard Jesse at the bathroom door when I was stepping out. "Breakfast is ready."

"Okay, I'll be right out." I combed my hair out quickly and threw on a cute cotton dress. Breakfast was at the table.

Pancakes, coffee, and juice. Perfect. Jesse pulled my chair out for me as I sat. I quickly kissed him on the cheek and turned his head and turned the sweet quick kiss into a long deep kiss. After he slowed us, he sat at his spot and took my hand in his. "Joey gets here tomorrow, right?"

"Right. Marco is getting him and his friend from the airport. They'll be here until next Saturday early in the morning. I know you have plans with Brie tomorrow night. I'm going to the barbecue and poker game. We are just hanging out on Saturday. Jenna's car needs some work done so we are going to do that in the morning. After that, it's a mellow hangout until we make dinner before going out to Rocky's. Sunday is up in the air depending on what time Gabby gets home from her mom's, but we will be having Sunday night dinner there. Mom will be home Wednesday and has already said Friday night is mandatory family dinner."

"It's going to be busy this week. Are you sure you want me at everything?"

He squeezed my hand slightly and ran his thumb across my thumb as he spoke. "Yes, just like I want you here all the time with me. I want you at whatever you want to be at and whatever you can be at."

"If I wasn't here, would you be coming home Friday night or sleeping there since you have to be up early to work on the car?"

"I'd be crashing on the couch."

"You should do that. Then you don't have to worry about driving. I can even drop you off on my way to Brie's and you can let me know when you're done with the car on Saturday and I'll come over."

"What about you on Friday night? Where will you be?"

"Here. This is home now, right?"

He leaned across the table and kissed me. "It sure is. Are you sure you don't want me to come home?"

"I want you home, but I think it's going to be a late night and an early morning. You'll get a lot more sleep if you stay."

"What if you drop me off, then when you're done with Brie, call me and I'll figure out what will be best? You're right, it's going to be a late night and an early morning."

"Tonight is our last night that it's the two of us until after Joey leaves. What do you want for dinner? I'm home so I'll cook dinner and when you get home, we can have a relaxing night the two of us."

"You have spoiled me with amazing food and made my favorite meal. Why don't you make your favorite? Plus, something chocolate for dessert."

"Sounds like a great plan."

"Any ideas of what else you want to do tonight?" There was that mischievous look again.

"I think I can come up with something. You'll just have to wait to find out when you get home. What time are you off?"

"Six no later than six-thirty. I have to close."

"Okay. I'll plan dinner for seven."

"I am going to head to work and I will see you tonight." He stood and started clearing his spot." Call me if you need me. I love you." He leaned down and kissed me before carrying his plate and glasses to the sink.

"I love you too. Don't forget your lunch. We didn't have leftovers yesterday since we were at your aunt's but there's other stuff still. Pick something. There's even pozole."

"I'm taking that."

"That's what I figured."

After he left, I finished my breakfast and cleaned the kitchen. I decided to call Brie and check in on tomorrow's plans. She picked up on the first ring.

"Hey, stranger. How are you enjoying having your place back to yourself?"

"Well, it's been an interesting couple of weeks. I'm glad we get to catch up tomorrow. I was calling to make sure we were still on for dinner tomorrow."

"Can we make it drinks at Rocky's? Danny and his friends are going there, so it would be a good mix."

"I don't want to go hang at Rocky's. We won't be able to visit. I need to talk to you and tell you what's been going on."

"We're talking now. You can tell me now. What's up?"

"It's fine. We can catch up another time. Let me know when you're free for lunch or dinner. Not Rocky's."

"Okay. Love you, Lex."

"Bye Brie."

Looks like I get a night to myself tomorrow. Me, a book, and a movie. I can handle that. When Jesse's done with Jenna's car stuff on Saturday, I can head over there. I can do this. I love Jesse. He wants me to be a part of his friends. I can do this.

I finished the crab apple tree painting and worked on my sketch for the show. I washed all the laundry and cleaned the bathroom and floors. I decided to prep dinner. Jesse told me to make my favorite dinner and my favorite dinner is appetizers and desserts. I put together a variety of appetizers - antipasto plate, veggie plate, cheese and crackers, homemade hummus, meatballs, and polenta bites. I made chocolate cheesecake with raspberry sauce for dessert. Right before six, I got a text from Jesse saying he should be closing right at six. I headed into the bedroom and changed. I decided that if it was date night, I was dressing for a date night even though we were staying home. I put on my favorite dress. It was emerald green, tight but comfortable, hit me mid-thigh, and was open back sitting at the small of my back. I was in the kitchen finishing the polenta bites when Jesse walked into the house.

He called out from the back door, "I'm home. My clothes are gross so they're going straight into the wash. I'm going to jump in the shower and then I'm all yours."

"Okay. I'm in the kitchen putting the final touches on dinner." I heard him less than a second before I felt him grab me by the waist and pull me toward him.

"Damn. You look amazing. So fancy for staying home?" He ran his finger along the small of my back as he kissed the back of my neck and across my shoulder.

"It's our last night for a week where it's us, so I decided to get fancy. Plus, I love this dress, but I've never worn it."

"You look beautiful." He spun me around and kissed me. "I'm going to go get fancy and I'll be right back."

He came back out 15 minutes later in black pants, a tucked-in black tailored button-up shirt with rolled sleeves to below his elbow, and black dress shoes. "What can I do to help?"

"You told me to make my favorite dinner. I made a variety of appetizers and a special dessert. We can set it on the kitchen counter buffet style. We'll have dessert later."

"I love it. Any other plans for tonight? Video games? Movie? More *NCIS*?"

"Poker."

"Best idea ever." He walked into the kitchen and pulled me into his side. "I stopped and checked out the painting before coming into the house. It's beautiful. Is it done?"

"It is."

"Did you decide where you want it?"

"The empty wall in the laundry room. I know it seems weird to put art in there, but it's the perfect size wall space for it since we can see the crabapple tree from the laundry room window."

"I think it's perfect on that wall. If it's dry and ready, I can hang it tonight."

"I still need to sign it. We can hang it later."

"Let me know when and I'll get it done. Now, tell me about all this amazing food."

"Meatballs with homemade sauce; polenta bites topped with sausage and veggies; homemade hummus with veggies; cheese and crackers; and antipasto. We have homemade chocolate cheesecake with raspberry sauce for dessert."

He wrapped his arms around my waist and pulled me in close to him. "Forget the week with Joey. I'm staying home, locking the doors, and never telling anyone where we are. So amazing Babe. Thank you." He kissed down the side of my neck and across my shoulder.

"You're welcome. You're fun to cook for because you appreciate everything. Even simple stuff like this." I turned my head and kissed him softly.

He handed me a plate. "Ladies first." I made my plate and headed to the table. He was right behind me to get my chair for me.

"Thanks."

"You're welcome."

We sat and ate for almost two hours. We've talked about everything already you'd think we'd run out of things to talk about, but we always find something. I told him about my conversation with Brie. "I can still take you and drop you off, so we only end up with one car, but I don't want to stay. It's too many people. I'll be there for the rest of the time."

"I get it. I'll drive and I can come to get you Saturday. I'll want to take a shower anyway. Pack a bag to stash in the trunk for the weekend so you have clothes and stuff. I usually do so I don't have to go back and forth."

"Okay. I'll get that together tomorrow night."

"What else are you going to do tomorrow?"

"I have a book to finish and I'm going to watch a super girly movie. The only thing I miss about my studio is being able to watch TV in bed. You only have the living room TV."

"We can get another TV, but I'm a big fan of the bedroom being for two activities only sleeping and-"

"*Pony* dancing."

He busted up. "Okay, three activities only."

"We do not need to buy a TV. I like the three activities rule for the bedroom. I'll watch my movie out here and read in bed when my movie is over."

"Sounds like a fun night. I might crash the end of it." He got up and cleared his plate. "That was so good. Do you want anything else?"

"No. Let's put it all away so we don't have to worry about it later. I used dishes that have lids. We just have to put lids on and put them in the fridge."

"You're a genius. Kitchen cleanup will only take me a few minutes. Do you want to get poker stuff set up?"

"Sure."

He joined me at the table a few minutes later. "This is a great date idea. Amazing food, a game we both love, and time together. Thank you."

"You're welcome." I handed him his share of the chips. "What game do you want to play or dealer's choice each hand?"

"Dealer's choice. What are we playing for Sweetheart?"

"Hmmm, I'm not sure. Got any ideas?"

There was that look again. "Only dirty ones."

I leaned across the table toward him. "Tell me."

"Winner picks location and position."

"Deal. I have lots of fun ideas and I've already proven I'm the better poker player."

"I almost want to fold now and find out more about those ideas Sweetheart, but I'm way too competitive for that. Deal the cards."

About an hour later, I had most of the chips. "Do you want a dessert break?"

"Yes. Definitely." He got up and got the cheesecake out of the fridge. "This looks amazing. Are you sure you aren't a professional chef?"

"You're sweet. I'm glad you like it. I made the raspberry sauce earlier; do you want me to warm it?"

He took a spoon, dipped it into the container, and tasted it. "This is amazing just like this." I sliced two slices and topped them with raspberry sauce. I handed him a plate and we headed to the couch to enjoy dessert. As soon as he took the first bite, he made the over the top moan. "I know I say this every time, but this is the best dessert ever." He reached his arm out and dragged me closer to him. "Thank you for everything and don't think I didn't notice that you cleaned the house today. Thank you." He kissed me, sweetly at first, but when I set my plate on the coffee table and moved in closer to him, he deepened the kiss and set his plate on the end table. "I give up. You win. Tell me what you want Sweetheart."

"Everything."

"You're not demanding at all, are you?" He pulled me closer.

"I didn't mean everything tonight, in general. Everything with you."

"Can I make a request for tonight?"

"Yes."

"I have never liked slow and sweet and I have never liked deep eye contact, but I want that again tonight."

"I'd like that again too. I want as much of you touching me again too. I want to feel you everywhere." He scooped me up and carried me to bed.

When we got to bed, he set me on my feet and whispered, "You're going to have to help me out here. Where is the zipper hidden? I've been looking for it and feeling for it all night. I can't find it. This dress is sexy as hell, but it needs to come off." I slid his hand from the small of my back to the zipper hidden on the side of the dress. He unzipped it and gently removed the dress. I reached for his shirt and started untucking it. He helped to make the process go faster. I reached for his belt and started unbuckling while he unbuttoned his shirt and removed it.

"Too many clothes. You have too many clothes, Jesse."

"Sorry Sweetheart. Next at-home date night let's plan to be naked from the start."

I giggled. "Deal." He set me on the edge of the foot of the bed. He kneeled in front of me. "What are you doing?" He pushed my thighs apart and leaned forward before taking me with his mouth. "Oh my God." He rotated between working over me with his mouth and his tongue and when I thought I couldn't stand it any longer, he took my clit in his mouth and sucked. "Holy shit Jesse." I slammed back onto the bed. "Wow. I changed my mind. I do like that. I've never liked that before. I think I'm going to like everything with you."

"I like that Sweetheart." He leaned down and kissed me. While he kissed me, he guided me further up the bed, so I was completely on the bed. I heard the crinkle of the condom wrapper and felt him slightly rotate so he could protect us without breaking the kiss. Once it was on, he lowered his voice. "Now for your request tonight - slow and sweet, eye contact, and as much of me touching you as possible. Anything else?"

"That's it."

"Roll onto your side, just like I am. Face me, scoot in close to me. As close as you can. I'm going to line up our hips." I did and he scooted me closer. He lifted my top leg and draped it over his. Lining up our hips had given him the perfect angle to slide into me.

"I didn't even know this was possible," I said as he began slowly rocking us. He did the forehead to forehead touch to get the deep eye contact and draped my arm over his side.

"Every part of you is touching me, Sweetheart. Do you need anything else?"

"Harder."

"You sure?" I nodded. "Tell me if it's too hard or fast. I'll fix it." I nodded again and started matching my rocking with his and we continued the eye contact.

Right when I was close, I said "harder and deeper." He lifted my leg slightly that was draped over his and rotated his position slightly so he could bury in me deeper and he thrust into me hard. I called out his name as everything went white.

"I like hearing you scream out my name." He pulled me toward him and scooted us to the top of the bed.

"Can't. Breathe." He pulled me up onto his chest and ran his fingers through my hair.

"Deep breath in Sweetheart and let it out slowly. Just breathe."

"I love you, Jesse."

"I love you too, Lexie. Thank you for tonight."

"You're welcome."

"Are you good?"

"Yeah."

"Let me up for a minute. I'll be right back. I need to deal with this."

When he returned to bed, he positioned us with me on his chest and I snuggled in close. He covered us with the blanket and the next thing I remember is waking up to his alarm. I started to get up. "Stay in bed Sweetheart. I can grab breakfast and I don't need lunch. We're closing at 12 so Marco can go to the airport. I'm coming home. I'll be fine."

"Grab some leftover stuff just in case."

"Or maybe to make the guys jealous." He winked at me while he was getting dressed. "What time are you done teaching?"

"11, I'll be home around 11:30."

"I'll be back here a little after noon. I need to be over at the house at three no later than four. Let's have lunch together."

"Sounds great. Do you want me to make anything for the barbecue?"

"No, Marco has everything planned. But thank you. I'll see you in a few hours. Have a good day teaching. I'll see you for lunch."

"I'll have everything ready. Text me when you're on your way home."

Chapter 11

Jesse

I could not wait to get home. We rarely closed the garage early and never closed on a Saturday, but Joey hadn't been home for over a year other than a quick stop before a guys' trip to Vegas for Marco's 30th birthday. We were closing at noon today and re-opening on Monday. I sent Lexie a text as I armed the building and headed home. I figured I'd find her in the kitchen. That was a routine I was getting used to. "Hey Sweetheart, I'm home," I called out as I was taking my boots off on the back patio.

"Hi. I'm in the kitchen."

"I was expecting that. Why are all the curtains and blinds closed? Is everything okay?"

"You said the next home date you wanted a naked date and naked isn't a good idea with open windows."

I bolted to the kitchen and found her putting last night's leftovers on plates for us. Completely naked. I walked over to her and wrapped my arms around her. "How hungry are you right now?"

"Not at all."

I guided her to the bedroom where we spent the rest of the afternoon. She was curled up in my arms when my phone rang.

"Hey, Joey! Welcome home!"

"Where are you?"

"Home."

"It's almost five you were supposed to be here at three, no later than four. Who is she?"

"Her name's Lexie and you'll meet her tomorrow. She's not big on large groups, almost like Jenna, but not quite as severe. I'll be on my way over soon." I hung up as Lexie started to wake.

"What time is it?"

"Close to five."

"You're late."

"I'm right where I'm supposed to be. I do need to get dressed and head over to Marco's. Are you sure you don't want to come?"

"I'm sure. I'm going to hang here, and I'll come over tomorrow. The plan's still you'll come over here to shower and get ready after you're done with Jenna's car?"

"Yes. We are hoping to be done no later than 11. I'll let you know."

"Okay." She wiggled her way out of my arms even though I tried to pull her back to me. She shook her head. "You need to get going."

I got dressed. "I put some stuff in that bag over there. There's room for your stuff if you want."

"Thanks. I'll put some stuff together, so I have it."

I grabbed her and pulled her close to me. "I'm going to miss you tonight. If I decide not to crash at Marco's, I'll let you know." She wrapped her arms over my shoulder and traced her fingers down my neck.

"Stay there. You'll be up late and need to be there early to work on Jenna's car. I'll be fine. I'll call you if I need anything. I promise." She pressed her body into mine and kissed me deeply.

"I love you. I'll see you tomorrow."

"I love you too. Have fun tonight."

The driveway was already crowded when I got there. I parked my bike in the back near the shop. As soon as I walked through the side gate, I saw Joey. "Hey man, welcome home."

"It's about time you got your ass here." He walked over to me and we broke the rule that guys don't hug. "Good to see you. Marco told me that you're basically in a relationship but calling it getting to know you."

I shook my head. "No, it's a full out relationship. She's amazing. She's smart, artistic, gorgeous, and for some reason, she actually wants to spend time with me. I gave her keys to the house a few days ago."

"She's the one you mentioned on the phone last month, right?" I nodded. "Damn! Pretty soon you're going to say three words you've never said before."

I grabbed a soda and popped it open. "Said it a few days ago. She means something, Joey. I never thought I was capable of this because I never had a model of what a healthy relationship should be. We started as friends. I was honest from the start that I don't do relationships. She got out of a messed up one about six months ago. We have a ton in common and she was fun to be with. Neither of us was looking for anything other than a friend to hang out with and someone to do stuff with. I figured out pretty quickly I didn't just want to be friends with her and was honest that I don't know how to do the relationship thing. She told me all I needed to do was what I already was doing and promise to only have my lips and hands on her. That was an easy request to honor because I don't want anyone else. Nothing has ever been like this. I can't not think about her."

"I can't wait to meet her. She grew up in town, right?"

"Yeah, but she's younger than us. She's a couple of years younger than Jenna. Her older sister graduated with Tony and they've known each other practically all their lives."

"I'm happy for you."

"Thanks. I recognize a lot of the people here from race days. Who's the tall blonde that could be Jenna's ex's twin?"

"My friend from my team. He had leave and didn't have plans. He's a good guy. I forgot how much he looked like Nick and you'll never believe this. His name's Nick."

"You're joking. You know that will send Jenna running home, right?"

"No, he's a good guy. I'd never bring trouble in the house. We're all used to going by our last name, so he's fine with being called Brady. Come on, I'll introduce you." We walked across the yard. "Hey, Brady! This is my other best friend, Jesse."

"Nice to meet you. You're the one in all the pictures in the house."

"Yeah. Marco is my cousin and I lived here growing up as much as with my mom or dad."

"Is the hot girl in the photos your sister or another cousin?"

"Neither. Jenna's 100% off-limits. I need to tell you that from the start. She'll be here later tonight. Stay away."

Joey added. "100% off-limits Brady."

"She's gorgeous and looks like she'd be fun for a week."

My big brother side came out. "Don't go there. We've all kicked an ass or two over Jenna including someone who used to be part of our group. I have no problem doing it again to someone I just met. She's off-limits."

I heard Marco's voice from behind me. "Who's off-limits?"

"Jenna." Joey and I respond at the same time.

"To everyone except me. She's my girl." He stepped up to Brady. "Stay away from her. First, because she's mine and second because you look similar to her piece of shit ex who I already took care of years ago."

Joey and I didn't say anything about Marco claiming Jenna as his. We both knew he was hoping for it eventually now that they're both single and Jenna's made some major progress getting over everything that happened in the last 10 years. I turned to Marco. "What do you need me to help with tonight?"

"Joey is taking care of chicken and manning the grill. Jenna will be here late because of traffic from the city. She'll do all the setup of stuff in the kitchen. I made most of the side stuff already. Keep on eye on the drink areas and do some walk-through in the house making sure there are no issues."

"Got it. What time do you want to start Jenna's car in the morning? I'm considering going home tonight and not crashing on the couch."

"Six no later than six-thirty. Not sure how much needs to be done and how long it will take but I know it's going to be hot tomorrow. I want to get it done. Any reason you don't want to stay here tonight or is it more a reason that you want to stay with someone else? Can I pick my extra two Saturdays off now?"

"I've got one that I can't take from you. I need to be at the end of summer festival. Go ahead and pick. Don't be an ass and make me work four in a row."

"You're going to the end of summer festival? I take Gabby to the kids' carnival area Friday night but never the event on Saturday."

"Lexie's art classes are having a student showcase and she's also showing some of her work in the art walk. I want to be there. It's a fundraiser to try to increase funding for additional art classes. She's coordinating the entire art show portion."

"Gabby was saying something about that. If she has stuff in the kids' show, I'll probably close the garage for the day. Give us both the opportunity to go to the festival. Take a look at your schedule and Lexie's and tell me what two in the next couple of months you're working for me. I don't need certain days off." He motioned for me to follow him. Once we were out of earshot from Brady and Joey, he finished his thought. "Keep an eye on Brady around Jenna. Joey says he's a bit of a player. He should take the hint now that all three of us have made it clear, but I don't want her uncomfortable this week."

"Already planning on it. She can always head to my place. She and Lexie get along and they've been texting since they met. They've even talked on the phone a couple of times. Jenna clued her on pozole being my favorite food, so Lexie made that the other night for dinner."

"You got two guestrooms now?" He smirked at me.

"Something like that."

"Happy for you."

"Thanks. I'll beer run with you later. Joey told me we needed to pick up other stuff. Had I known, I would have driven my car instead of the bike." I headed off to find Joey and get our catch up started.

A couple of hours later, the yard was packed with about thirty people from our racing days. I walked through the house and made sure no one was where they shouldn't be. I had left Jenna and Joey out by the grill playing catch up. Suddenly Jenna stormed into the house, grabbed Marco by the shirt, and pulled him into the laundry room. I sat on the couch and called Lexie.

"Hey Sweetheart, I wanted to check-in. How's your night going?"

"Good. I just finished a movie and I'm going to start a second one. I'm going to go be a bed hog and read in bed and sleep in the middle of that giant bed. How's the party?"

"Loud and crowded. Are you sure you don't want me to come home tonight? I haven't had a beer yet in case you wanted me to drive home."

"It's easier if you stay. You'll get more sleep, and you can enjoy yourself and not have to drive. I'll see you tomorrow afternoon and I'll go back to the house with you. Have fun tonight and win that poker game."

"Hoping to. Enjoy your night. I love you."

"I love you too." I hung up after she did.

I heard Jenna and Marco in the laundry room and saw Joey pulling chicken off the grill. I walked over and knocked on the pocket door. "Chicken's ready. Might want to stop whatever you're doing in there and give Jenna a chance to catch her breath before anyone else comes inside to fill plates. I could hear her from the living room." I heard Jenna's giggles and Marco's laugh as I walked away from the door. Maybe they were finally figuring out they were supposed to be together. They've been tiptoeing around it for so long.

After the ladies got dinner, I filled my plate and went out to the picnic table to join Jenna and Marco. Joey and Brady joined us a few minutes later. Marco asked, "Any special requests while you're home?"

"I already promised Gabby I'd do something with her every day. Other than that, I want to hang out. Maybe go to the shop one day, get my hands on a car or two. I miss it."

Marco laughed. "Well, you're in luck. We need to work on Jenna's tomorrow, so I'm recruiting all of you to help so we are done before it's hot. Tony's working the bar at Rocky's tomorrow so we can go there."

"Perfect. I figure everything else will fall into place while I'm home."

Joey had turned on his famous everything 90s mix playlist. When *Motownphilly* was followed by *Runaway Train* and *Red Light Special,* Jenna burst into laughter. "Seriously Joey? *Boyz II Men, Soul Asylum,* and *TLC* don't belong in a triple play. Is there any sort of theme to this mix or is it every 90s song you like?"

"Don't go music snob on me Baby Girl. I taught you everything you know about good music. The theme is the 90s. It doesn't need anything else." Joey replied.

"I don't know what's more ridiculous the four of you straddled across the bench at this table because you don't fit to sit at it or the randomness of this playlist."

Brady said, "I thought this fool," pointing toward Joey "was tall and then I showed up here and met these two."

"Tell me about it. Joey left for the Army at six-foot two-inches and came back with an extra inch; Jesse has been six-three since I was 14; Marco is close to six-six." She turned to Marco. "Why did you buy a picnic table that you can't sit at and have to straddle instead of a table with chairs?"

"Because it's what you and Gabby asked for." He said it without skipping a beat between bites of food.

"That's sweet. I didn't realize that. Thank you." She leaned over and kissed him on the cheek.

"Gross. Kissing. Gross." Joey said in his fake high pitch voice.

Jenna glared at him. "I know why you're doing that. I know I was an obnoxious bratty little sister that you were all stuck with and I ruined lots of kissing moments for you when girls were around. This is payback. I'm ready for all the teasing and comments." Jenna was practically falling asleep leaning on Marco. He told her to go to bed and he'd see her in the morning after we were done working on her car in the shop. "I'm going to call it a night. You guys have fun playing poker. I'll see you in the morning." She headed to bed.

I cleared the picnic table and grabbed a trash bag. "I'll clean up the yard. Joey, can you take care of the grill? Sounds like Marco promised Jenna he'd take care of dishes, so I'm leaving him with kitchen clean up. We can get that done and play some poker."

Once everything was cleaned up and most of the race friends had left, we set up the poker game. We didn't start the game until almost midnight. I got a text from Lexie right after the game started.

> I'm going to sleep now. Goodnight. I hope you are having a fun night.
>
> It's been good catching up. I miss you. I've been thinking about you non-stop.
>
> I miss you too. I always think about you non-stop.
>
> Sleep well Sweetheart. I'll see you tomorrow as soon as Jenna's car is done.
>
> Win that poker game. Goodnight.

Our winner takes all poker game was down to me and Brady. It was close to three. There was no way I was losing this game. I forced him all in on what I knew was a bluff and took the win. I grabbed a pillow from the hall closet and a blanket and crashed on my usual couch spot. My alarm went off at six to wake everyone to work on the car, there's no way. Way too tired. I knocked on Marco's door.

"Fuckin' Jesse." Marco moaned as he woke. I heard Jenna laugh.

"Just letting you know I'm in no shape to work on the car yet. I'll wake you in two hours."

"Okay."

I woke everyone at eight and we headed out to the shop at the back of the property to work on Jenna's car.

"Marco, we can't keep fixing it. It's crap. When are you going to tell her about the Honda?" I asked.

"Soon. I need her a little more comfortable driving it. She's been driving it a lot since I put Gabby's car seat in it."

Joey asked, "what Honda?"

"The blue one. I got a sweet deal on it. We fixed it up and I told Jenna I got it so there was one car for whoever had Gabby, so we didn't need to do the car seat shuffle."

"How's she doing driving?" Joey asked.

Marco shrugged. "So so. It's better, but the drive from the city is hard."

Marco assigned jobs out to everyone to make the work faster. About an hour and a half into the work, we heard Jenna enter the garage. "Hey guys, I made breakfast. Fried egg sandwiches, a blender full of mixed berry smoothie, and coffee." Worked stopped and we all grabbed food. I grabbed a chair and my phone to text Lexie while I ate.

Good morning Sweetheart. I just wanted to text and say I love you.

Good morning. I love you too. How'd you sleep?

Not as well as I do with you.

Same.

We are about halfway done with the work. I should be home in about two hours. I'll shower and we can head back over. It's movies and hanging out this afternoon. Rocky's for dancing after we BBQ dinner.

I'll see you in a couple of hours.

I'll let you know when I'm on my way home.

Okay. I'm sure you know where I'll be.

Studio or kitchen.

Or the shower.

Save that for when I'm home. We can share.

My favorite kind of shower.

Mine too.

Joey tapped me on the shoulder. "Are you planning on texting while we do all the work or are you joining us?"

"Sorry. I got a little distracted. Let's get this done. Marco, I'm thinking very basics and try to get her to start driving the Honda since she's here this week."

"That's my plan." Marco finished what he was working on and then finished helping Brady with tires.

We were done sooner than I expected so I was able to head home almost an hour early. Lexie wasn't in the studio when I got there. I left my boots at the door and opened the back door. "You better not be in the shower already," I called out as I stepped into the house.

"I'm not." I heard her voice coming from the laundry room. I stepped in. She stepped toward me and I pulled her in close and kissed her.

"I missed you last night, Sweetheart. I missed sleeping with my arms wrapped around you and I missed waking up with you in my arms."

"I missed all of that too." She bit her lower lip.

I brought my mouth down to her ear and whispered. "Tell me. I know you're holding something in. Tell me."

"I missed-" she stopped.

"What did you miss?" She did the lip thing. "Tell me. What did you miss?"

"I missed you."

"You already said that." I put my forehead on hers.

"I missed being with you." She emphasized the word 'being.'

"You missed me being buried deep inside you. Is that what you were trying to say?"

"Yes, that. Okay. I can't say things like that. But it's definitely what I was thinking."

"I missed that too. It happens to be something we can take care of before we head back to the house. Music to stop the mind spin, eye contact, anything else?"

She leaned forward and whispered, "pin me against the shower wall."

I scooped her up and carried her toward the bedroom. She wrapped her legs around my waist and ground against me. "Slow Baby. No rush."

She shook her head. "Now. I want you fast and hard. I want you now. You said it was my pace and I want fast and hard."

I stopped in the doorway and pinned her against the door frame. "Tell me if you want me to stop." I reached under her nightgown and began working her with my finger. "So wet already."

She took my ear in her mouth and nibbled on it. "Always. Only for you. I've never reacted like this before." I knew she needed fast so I applied pressure on her clit and worked my fingers in and out of her quickly she started to clench and traced up the wall to the G and she threw her head back and screamed out my name as she clenched harder around me. I took my fingers out of her and repositioned her over my shoulder and walked into the bathroom. I turned the water on, and we quickly undressed. I set my phone on the dock and turned on the playlist and flipped the ringer off, so we weren't interrupted. I stepped in the shower first and pulled her in with me.

I pulled her in close to me and wrapped my arms around her waist. I placed my forehead on hers. "Hard, fast, and pinned against the wall. Eye contact and music to block the mind spin. Anything else?"

She nodded her head. "Now!"

I backed her up to the wall and placed one hand over her head against the wall and kept the other on her hip. I leaned down and took her mouth with mine. I slowly pulled back. "Tell me if you need me to stop." She nodded. I took her lips again and she parted allowing me in. I took my hand that was on her hip and ran it down the back of her leg to mid-thigh and guided it up to rest on my upper thigh. "Leave it here." She nodded.

"Now Jesse. Now."

I slammed into her hard and fast. Her arms moved over my shoulders and linked behind my neck. I pulled her leg from my thigh up higher to my hip and stepped closer to her allowing me to slam deeper into her and pinned her tighter against the wall. "Good?"

"So good. Harder."

I slammed into her harder and she wrapped her arms and leg around me tighter. I leaned down and whispered "Is this what you were dreaming about in our bed last night? Me buried deep in you and slamming you this hard." She nodded and I slammed one more time and she screamed out my name as she clenched hard around me and I kept going. I picked her up by the back of her thighs and guided her to wrap tight around me and pressed her against the wall. I finished with her name on my lips and gently set her down.

She wrapped her arms around my waist, and I pulled her close, resting my chin on top of her head. "Thank you, Jesse. That was better than I dreamed of."

"You're welcome, Sweetheart. Everything, remember? I'm going to give you everything you want while making all the bad memories disappear." I turned off the water, opened the door, and grabbed a towel. I wrapped her in the towel and carried her to our bed. I placed her in the center of the bed and crawled up next to her. "When you're ready, we need to talk about something."

"Good something or bad something?"

"Neutral."

"Okay. I'm ready."

"I realized when I turned the water off that we had the birth control conversation, but we never had the no condom discussion and we obviously didn't use one in the shower. I should have asked you if you were okay with that first. I'm sorry. I should have asked. I've never not before. You know that."

"I knew when I told you I wanted the shower. I could have asked too. I knew. I'm on the pill. We're good. We know each other's histories. I'm fine with no condoms if you are."

"You're sure?"

"Yes, I'm sure."

I pulled her close to me and we both drifted to sleep. We woke twenty minutes later and got dressed and grabbed our stuff for the rest of the weekend and headed to Marco's.

Chapter 12

Lexie

Jesse parked his car in the driveway next to Marco's truck and behind the red Honda, not the one we had traded cars for, but the other one. I looked at him and quietly asked, "why am I so nervous? I've been here before."

Jesse reached for my hand. "I've got you. You know Jenna and Marco already. Tony will be around every once in a while. Shauna will be here, and you'll love her. She's sweet like Jenna but loud and opinionated. Joey is super laid back. His friend Brady seems like a good guy." He leaned across the front seat and kissed me sweetly before getting out of the car and coming around to my door. He took my hand. "Come on, let's go hang out."

We walked in the front door and I found a room full of people I've never seen before. "Everyone, this is Lexie. Lexie this is everyone. Joey, Brady, and Shauna. Where are Marco and Jenna?"

Joey replied, "they left right after you left to go grab paperwork at the garage so Marco could finish payroll. They're not back."

"That should take ten minutes, an hour if they did payroll there. It's been almost two hours. I'm calling them." Marco's phone went to voicemail. So did Jenna's. They didn't answer at the shop. He looked at Joey. "You call Marco, I'll call Jenna. If the phones ring at the same time they might stop ignoring us."

Jenna picked up. "Where are you?" I couldn't hear what she said before he replied "Okay, payroll pick up takes ten minutes tops. It's been over two hours." He laughed when he hung up the phone. "They're on their way back." He took my hand and led me over to the L-shaped couch.

Shauna looked over at me. "Hi. It's nice to finally meet you. Jesse tells me nothing, ever, but Jenna's been my best friend since we were three. She told me she met you a couple of weeks ago and that you kicked everyone's ass at poker. I am so sad I missed it. It's always Marco and Tony as the final two. I would have paid to see you win."

"Thanks. It's nice to meet you too. Jesse won last night's game."

"Marco is not going to be happy about two losses in a row. That never happens. I think I need poker lessons from you." Jesse was right. Shauna was nice.

"We could totally do that. Maybe a girls' poker day, get Jenna to join us."

"That would be so much fun. I also heard you are a reader. I know the owner of the bookstore and she said you are in at least once a week."

"Checking up on me?"

"More like looking out for you. We all know Jesse isn't a relationship guy and I just wanted to know more about you."

"We both went into this not wanting a relationship. I got out of a messed up relationship about six months ago. I grew up here. I know his reputation. We have a ton in common and have fun together. We started as friends, just hanging out. It's become more. We are both seeing where it goes."

"I like it. I like you two together."

Jesse leaned over and whispered to me. "I like us together too." He got up to grab drinks from the kitchen. "Does anyone want anything?"

"Water." Shauna and I both asked at the same time. He brought us both a water and sat back down on the couch next to me, placing his hand on my waist and scooted me toward him.

"So, what are the plans for the rest of the day?" I asked as I snuggled in close to him.

"The guys are exhausted after a late poker game and party clean up, then being up early to fix Jenna's car, so it's a movie afternoon and dinner. After that, we are going to Rocky's. Jenna and I will dance, and we will make Joey dance since he knows all the dances, and the guys will drink and catch up. Do you dance?"

"Sounds great. I love to dance." I turned to look at Jesse. "Do you dance?"

"I know a few of the dances, but I usually just hang at a table." He lowered his voice and whispered in my ear. "I might be willing to make an exception for you. We already know you like my dancing Sweetheart."

I leaned up to his ear and whispered where no one else could hear me. "I think your dancing is sexy."

"Okay, I'll dance." He positioned us on the couch so I could lean against him and he had his arms wrapped around my waist.

Shauna laughed. "I don't think I even want to know what you said to him, but part of me does, because you will quickly learn I'm the girl who wants to know all the dirty details. Always." I laughed.

Just then Jenna came running through the door, looked at Shauna, and said, "Sorry, we were at the garage getting paperwork stuff done that needed to be done before Monday."

"I got off early and headed over and from the looks of you, you had a lot of paperwork to do." She put air quotes around the word paperwork. Jenna headed down the hall and Shauna followed.

I turned to look at Jesse. "I think I'm going to like Shauna and I already like Jenna."

"I told you. You're going to get along great with both of them. Can you help me in the kitchen for a minute? I'll put snacks out for the movie, and we can claim our spot back on the couch. It's the most comfortable. I will probably fall asleep during the movie because I slept like shit last night."

"Sure." I followed him into the kitchen. "I slept awful too. I missed you. It's only been a few nights and I've already gotten to the point I can't sleep without you."

He pulled me close and hugged me. He placed his mouth on my ear. "I've gotten used to sleeping with you too and one night away was too much. I'm not planning on a night away ever again." He placed a kiss on the side of my neck before letting me go. We grabbed bowls for chips and pretzels, set those on the coffee table, and claimed the couch. Marco came in as we finished setting out snacks.

"Hey Lexie, glad you made it. You're going out with us tonight too, right?"

"Yeah, I'm around the rest of the weekend. Let me know if I can help with anything. Jesse said something about dinner tonight and breakfast tomorrow and maybe Sunday dinner if Gabby wants one."

"She'll want one. I'm sure Jenna would love help with food."

"Okay. I can help. I love to cook."

"I've been smelling the leftovers he's been taunting us with at work. Just from the smells and looks of everything, you're a great cook."

"Thanks." I turned to look at Jesse. "With all that food, you didn't share anything, did you?"

"Nope. I ate it all. Even the desserts you packed for me to share. I ate every bite myself."

"You are bad. I have another week before classes start back in the city. I'll have to bring lunch in for everyone one day."

Joey chimed in, "Make sure it's a day I'm hanging out, please. One of the first things I heard about you from Jesse was that you were artistically talented and a great cook. He said you could kick his ass at video games and poker. I swear I didn't believe you were real until you walked through the door."

"Thanks. I'll be sure to cook before you leave." Jesse pulled me in closer to him. He was sitting with his back against the part of the couch that meets forming the L. He rotated so I could lay next to him resting against his chest. "You were right, this couch is super comfy. I'm going to fall asleep during the movie."

He leaned in and whispered, "I told you it was the best spot. We're claiming it all weekend. I slept here last night, but it's more comfortable now that you're here."

Marco sat in his chair and put his feet up on the ottoman. He started flipping through movies and asked what anyone wanted to watch. No one responded. Joey was stretched out on the floor. Shauna was on the other side of the L-shape couch. Brady was on the small couch and Jenna came in and curled into the chair with Marco.

Marco said, "Someone needs to pick something or I'm letting the girls decide and we are going to end up watching some Nicholas Sparks bullshit." Jenna, Shauna, and I all say, "*A Walk to Remember*." The guys groaned and we burst into laughter.

Brady glanced around and said, "I must be missing a story."

Jenna told the story about the history of the movie that Jesse had told me the night I was reading the book.

"Never seen it. I think we should watch it." Brady said with a laugh.

"Yes, let's do it," I said. Jesse tucked me in closer to his side and placed kisses down my neck.

Joey sat up from where he had been sprawled out on the floor. "Oh hell no. Not happening babes. I did not come home to watch some Nicholas Sparks bullshit. I only watch that stuff when I have a chance of getting laid and two of the girls are taken and one is family. I'm calling veto. Give me the remote."

"Gladly." Marco threw it across the living room to him.

"Which one of the girls is family?" Brady asked as he looked between the three of us.

"Shauna's mom married my dad about nine years ago. They divorced three years ago, but we lived in the same house for years before they married, so we are basically siblings and grew up together."

Jesse slightly propped himself up to see Brady. "You'll quickly learn Woods Lake has grown a lot and become the suburb to the city but when we were growing up it was still pretty small, and all of our parents grew up here as well as most of our grandparents. Most of us can connect back to at least one if not two people in the room. Jenna and I were almost related at one time and she's currently related to Shauna."

Shauna told the rest of the story. "It's true and it's probably the most fucked up of all the stories. My dad and her mom met when we were three. My family moved in across the street from Jenna's family. Her mom and dad were still married. My parents were still married. Our parents got divorced about a year after her mom and my dad walked out on all of us and never looked back. They're married now with three new kids and we haven't seen them in over twenty years."

"Holy shit. Jesse, how do you fit into this?"

"My mom dated Jenna's dad for about a year, got engaged to him, and we lived in their house for about nine months before my mom realized what a truly fucked up bastard he was and got the hell out."

"Pick a movie or I'm going to agree to the Nicholas Sparks bullshit," Marco said.

"What about Marco? How do you fit into the family?" Brady asked as he turned to look at Marco and Jenna.

"My dad and Jesse's dad are brothers. We are literally family."

"Damn. Small towns are twisted." Brady said as he stretched out on the couch.

"That's not even the half of it man. You practically need to check a family tree before you ask someone out." Joey said from the floor. "I found it. *Days of Thunder*. Race cars for us and Tom Cruise for the girls. It's a hell of a lot better than a Nicholas Sparks movie and isn't on our list of banned race theme movies." He hit play.

Jenna looked at me. "Jesse told me you're a reader too and you have the same rule about being sure to see movies only after reading the book. You'll have to join us for our next book and movie adventure."

"I'd love that."

Less than five minutes into the movie, Jesse wrapped me in his arms tightly and scooted us down the couch. He whispered in my ear. "Sleep. The nap this afternoon wasn't nearly long enough. Sleep." I turned so I was facing him and snuggled in using his shoulder as a pillow.

I woke up a little after six. I hadn't moved, but Jesse had thrown his leg over me pinning me in place against him. I'm usually a huge fan of personal space and separate sides of the bed when sleeping. I would have never snuggled in on a couch with anyone before Jesse, but this felt completely natural and right. I knew he was still tired and didn't hear anyone else around, so I stayed exactly where I was and just enjoyed it. About twenty minutes later he started to stir. "Hey sleepyhead, did you have a good nap?" I asked as I leaned up to kiss him on the cheek. He turned and changed the sweet cheek kiss I intended into a deep kiss when he captured my lips.

"Best nap ever. How'd you sleep?"

"So good. What are the plans tonight? Should we help with dinner?"

"Yeah, let me get up and see the status of things."

We heard Shauna knocking on Marco's bedroom door. "It's almost seven. Joey started the grill. I'm supposed to find out what else we are having with dinner."

Jesse laughed. "We're going to need to get up. If Joey recruited Shauna's help with dinner we're screwed. She can't make toast. She burned a pot of boiling water at Jenna's apartment a couple of weeks ago."

"Yikes. Let me up and I'll go help."

Marco had come down the hall and was starting to get stuff together in the kitchen. Jenna came out a couple of minutes later. I went into the kitchen and started pulling the leftovers out. "I'll get leftover stuff ready." I looked over at Jenna and lowered my voice. "I like the two of you together."

She smiled at me. "Thanks. I like the two of you together too. I'm glad you're here."

"Thanks. I know the reputation, but I think there's potential here."

She nodded her head and before she could respond, Jesse wrapped his arm around my waist. "There is Sweetheart. I want you where I am. This is new for me and I might totally fuck up and forget to tell you I want you here, but I do." He lowered his voice so only I could hear him. "I think I've made it clear at home when it's only the two of us, but I wanted to be sure you knew that I want you here with my friends too. This group, minus Brady, plus Marco's mom, Gabby, Tony, and Rocky, and that's my entire family. I want you here."

I nodded and turned to face him and mouthed "I know." He kissed me sweetly.

Jenna smiled at me and said, "Lexie, after we get dinner stuff prepped, let me show where I keep all the girly stuff in this giant man cave, that way you'll know in case you need anything. I'm sure you've figured out this is essentially base camp for our friends. I'm glad you'll be around more."

"Thanks, me too." Jesse's chin was resting on my shoulder and he had his arms wrapped around my waist holding me close to him. I looked back at him again. "You either need to help me or let me go. I want to help Jenna get things ready."

Brady brought in the burgers. "Burgers are ready. What are the plans for the rest of the night?"

Jenna let him know the plans for after dinner and we figured out cars and drivers. Marco and Jenna were riding alone in case she wanted to come home early. She was most comfortable driving the Honda, so they were taking that. Marco's truck was off-limits to anyone to drive. That left Jesse's car and Shauna's since everything else was blocked in. "Jesse can drive to Rocky's and I can drive back. I don't mind driving."

Shauna said, "we need one more driver unless we want to pile in the backseat, and I don't think any of the guys will fit with three in the backseat. I don't mind driving. We can do a girl's drive night and next time it's our turn."

"Works for me." Jesse nudged me to go through the dinner line and grab food. "Ladies first, always." He winked at me.

I kissed him on the cheek and whispered, "I'm really liking that rule."

I grabbed drinks for both of us and took them to the table. Jesse scooted my chair closer to him when he got to the table. "Thanks for grabbing my drink." He leaned in to whisper something to me, but before he could, Joey chimed in.

"Okay, I'm just going to say it, because everyone else is thinking it. Lexie, how did you get him to settle down? He's been firmly a no relationship guy since high school. About a month ago, I called to catch up with him and he wouldn't shut up about this amazing girl who he can't get out of his mind. I figured it's going to pass, and I wouldn't meet you this trip, but here you are, and we all want to know how you did it."

All eyes are on me. "Well, it just started with a friendship. We ran into each other at Rocky's last month and he saved me from having to spend time with my sister's awful friends. He told me that he bought my favorite house in town and invited me over to see it since I was so excited about it. I got out of an awful relationship about six months ago and it should have been over a long time ago. I was firmly in the 'all men are assholes camp' and not looking for anything. We found out that we are both highly competitive; video game nerds; love poker; and have a massive, sweet tooth. I think I won him over when I told him that I'm the type of girl who eats brownies straight out of the pan."

"She did. I've never met anyone who is this smart and talented. She keeps me on toes, and we have fun. There's never been anyone that I have this much fun with. I think because we both started in the no relationship mindset, we were able to just have fun and be friends with no pressure. The more I spent time with her, the more I wanted to spend more time with her, and suddenly I'm telling her that I have no idea how to be a boyfriend, but I wanted to figure out." He reached his hand over and put his hand on my thigh under the table.

"Damn. I never thought I'd see this day and it's amazing. I'm happy for you both." Joey said as he looked across the table at us. Jenna and Shauna were both sharing glances back and forth with each other and then me.

Jenna announced, "girls are driving tonight, so that means we don't have to do dishes." She stood up and looked at me. "Do you have clothes for tonight? If not, I'm sure between Shauna and me, we have stuff."

"I have a bag in the car."

"Go get it and meet us in the big bathroom. We are taking over Marco's room to get ready while the guys clean up."

Jesse asked, "since when is this a rule that guys clean up when the girls drive?"

Jenna laughed. "Since now. I just made it up. Next time, it will be guys clean up while we get ready just because, so just deal with it. It takes us longer to get ready than you."

She and Shauna walked down the hall and Jesse went out to the car to grab our bag, before leading me down the hall. "Dinner conversation got a bit intense. Are you good?"

"I'm great. I really am. I think everyone has noticed that we moved fast and I'm okay with that." He pulled me in close kissed me sweetly, opened the bedroom door, and dropped our bag on the bed.

"I just need my jeans and shirt, so I'll grab that, and I'll be out of here."

I joined Jenna and Shauna in the bathroom. "Wow. This bathroom is huge and fancy. I could swim in that tub." I stopped in the bathroom doorway to check it out before walking the rest of the way in.

Jenna turned and looked at me. "Right? It's my favorite part of the addition. I told him that I am using this tub every day when I'm here this week. At first, I thought the walk-in closet in the bathroom was a weird idea, but it makes getting ready so much easier and I swear that the bathroom and closet are bigger than my apartment."

I laid out my make up on the counter. "What are you both wearing tonight? I was going with jeans, boots, and a cute top. You're not the girls that do fancy dresses for line dancing, are you?"

"We definitely aren't. Shauna owns some awesome dresses, but not for Rocky's."

"Oh, good gracious no. Definitely not." Shauna had finished straightening her hair. "Does anyone need a flat iron?" Jenna and I both shook our heads.

"Jesse said the three of us would get along great. He was right. I'm usually shy and it takes me forever to get comfortable with people, so thank you for being so welcoming"

"I think it's pretty obvious that I'm shy and hardly talk to new people, so this group is okay with that and seriously Jesse never brings girls around. A big party he might have someone there, but not to movie afternoons or dinners. That has never happened. I've known him since I was twelve and I've never seen him with the same girl twice." Jenna was jabbering on and super talkative. That was a good sign that we were going to get along.

"Okay, we aren't making him sound good," Shauna said as she was digging through her makeup bag. "Jesse is amazing. He's a great guy. He just never had a good relationship model. Not like most of us did, but we at least had something."

"You don't have to sell me on. He's the greatest guy I've ever met and the only one to treat me nice. Before him, I've never heard any sort of kind words."

Jenna looked at me. "Sounds familiar. I dated someone who used to be pretty tight in our group. My thought process was if the guys who loved me like a sister and my brother liked him, then he must be a good guy. Turns out he wasn't. Nick was a monster. Everything about our relationship was on his terms. He cheated a lot but denied it and made me think I was losing my mind. He was abusive physically and emotionally. Every part of a relationship that is supposed to feel good was painful. I didn't know what a relationship should be because my mom walked out when I was four and my dad had a series of "friends" and eventually Jesse's mom, but she was smart and got out fast. Marco's dad died just after I met him. I didn't have them as a relationship model for long." Shauna reached over and hugged Jenna.

"Sounds a lot like what I just got out of and am still dealing with when Kyle randomly shows up. Thankfully, Jesse was there the last time he showed."

"Marco told me a little about that. We have similar pasts, so I think we will both understand that sometimes we just can't share. It's not that we don't want to but can't."

"Exactly. I completely understand that." I finished my makeup and hair while we talked. I paused for a moment. "Jenna, can I ask you something else?"

"Since you're going to be around more, I'm going to let you know that you can ask me anything, but I may not answer. Does that make sense?"

"Yeah. I get it. We have a lot in common about our fucked-up pasts. Sounds like our dads would have gotten along great and I have no fucking idea where my mom is."

"You get it. Go ahead and ask?"

"Why the flip with you and Marco? I was here a couple of weeks ago, and you were in the 'just friends camp', now it's a complete one-eighty. What changed?"

"He convinced me to give it a one-week trial run since I was staying here to have more time with Joey. Within twelve hours of faking it, it feels more real than anything I've ever had so I decided to give us a real chance. He's made it clear that he wants it to be real and has wanted it to be real for a long time. I think everyone knows that he was my childhood crush and the person who I compare everyone to. He's also been the only consistent safe person in my life, so I'm risking a lot if this doesn't work, but he promised that if I decide a relationship doesn't work that he'll always still be there. I told him this afternoon that I'm in completely, and I'm going to give us a real chance."

"I think it's great. I've thought since I met you that you should be together. Jesse let me know that when your brother died and your dad lost it, you ended up living here, so the history makes it hard. I hope you don't mind he told me."

"Me growing up in this house isn't a secret. There are pictures everywhere. Most people think I'm a sister or cousin based on the photos. Marco's mom is the only parent I've had since my mom walked out when I was four. Mom took me in as soon as I met her when I was twelve and tried to make up for the eight years. She had all the talks that moms are supposed to have with their daughters. She sat through all the tears from broken hearts. She tried to keep me from following the race life path that the guys were firmly down, but it was too late. I was already crazy about fast cars and motorcycles. I wanted to be where my brother was and not be home at night, so I felt safer out at the race and the parties that followed than I did in the house. She made sure Marco made sure I had everything I needed to stay as safe as possible and I wasn't allowed to go anywhere without at least two out of the four guys there to keep an eye on me."

"She sounds pretty awesome. I hope I get to meet her."

"You will. Jesse grew up in this house too, so he's here a lot which means you will be here. She will love you. She's on a church retreat; otherwise, we'd be having Sunday night dinner tomorrow. It's mandatory for all of us and whoever we are dating is invited as are any friends who want to be here. Gabby will be home in the afternoon and will likely want a mini version, so you'll be here for that."

"Wow. That sounds great. I can't remember the last time I had a family dinner. Meals here are the closest I've had in years. I already let Marco know that I'm willing to help you guys cook meals this weekend and week while I'm around. Just let me know what you need."

"Well, now you're here every Sunday and unless Shauna's working, she's here. Us girls have to stick together. I've been the only constant girl in this group for a long time. I will take you up on that offer to help with food. Marco said something about Jesse suddenly having fancy leftover lunches. How often have you been cooking for him?"

"Almost daily. I'm sure you know that I was sort of forced to move into the guest room for a few days because of issues with Kyle and the guys, meaning Jesse, Tony, and Marco, don't want me at my apartment until they know he's gone. I have a couple of weeks I'm not teaching classes in the city, so I've been cooking a lot."

"You're going to spoil him and he's not going to want you to leave," Shauna said as she finished her makeup. Jenna winked at me and I had a feeling she'd already heard more about our plans from Marco than anyone else.

I heard the bedroom door open. "Hey Babe, I need clothes. Are you dressed?" Marco called from the bedroom door.

"They are, but I'm completely naked," Jenna said while trying to contain laughter.

Shauna and I started laughing. "Don't tease me. You won't make it out of this room to go dancing tonight."

"Yes, we are dressed. You can come in and grab clothes."

Shauna and I left to go change in Gabby's room so Marco could get ready.

I found Jesse on his favorite spot on the couch. He stood up when I came into the room. "You look beautiful." He reached out and pulled me into him. He lowered his voice. "Shauna can drive Brady and Joey back here and we can stay at home tonight or we can just skip Rocky's completely."

I whispered, "We're going dancing. You promised you'd dance. We can stay at the house and just come back here early. I told Jenna I could help with food prep stuff for tomorrow for breakfast and family dinner."

"Alright, let's go get our dance on." Then he called out a little louder. "Let's go. We're taking my car, Shauna has the soldiers, and Marco and Jenna are in the Honda. Last one there buys the first round."

Joey called out, "Shauna give me your keys. I know I'm a better driver."

We bolted out the door and to Jesse's car. Even with the first round on the line, he opened my door for me and made sure I was in before closing it. We parked in the parking lot at Rocky's and ran for the door, bypassing the line of people waiting to get it. "Hey tío, looks busy tonight," Jesse said as we approached the door.

"It is. So, this," pointing to the two of us, "is still going on?" We nodded. "I like it. I like it a lot. Lexie, I think you're good for him. The corner table area in the back is reserved for you. Have fun tonight. Let me know if you guys need anything."

We were in the door just before Joey, Brady, and Shauna walked in. "First round is on me." Joey walked up to the bar. "Lexie, what do you want?"

"I'm driving, so I'm good."

"She'll take a club soda with lime. I'll take whatever lager is on tap." He pulled me close to him. "Let's go dance."

Shauna found us on the dance floor a little while later. "You're a miracle worker girl. He has known all the dances for years but will never dance. How'd you convince him?"

"Chocolate. He'll do anything if I promise to bake." Jesse started laughing. A few minutes later Jenna joined us and so did Joey. "Anyone else dancing?" I asked as I looked at the table.

"No. Marco knows one dance and might dance that but only with Jenna. Jesse never dances, so you're working miracles. Brady knows them all. He grew up outside of Nashville, so country is in his bones. Find him a beautiful girl and he'll spend the night on the dance floor; otherwise, he'll be at the bar." Joey answered as he quickly taught me the steps to the dance I didn't know.

A partner dance came on and everyone started to clear the floor, except us. "Come here, Sweetheart. I know this one. Do you?" I shook my head. "I'll teach you." I saw Joey pull Jenna back onto the dance floor.

"What's their story? They seem like more than a lifetime friendship."

"Joey and Shauna lived across the street from Jenna and Ricky and when things got bad in that house, Joey made sure Jenna was safe. He, Ricky, and Marco were the three amigos growing up. I was in and out of the group depending on if I was living with my aunt or one of my parents. That bond is unbreakable."

"I think it's great that you've all stayed so close."

"What about you? Any lifelong childhood friends?"

"No. I was the weird art girl. My sister and I were raising ourselves. I don't even know how we had our own place starting at fourteen and sixteen, but we did. We both worked a lot in school because we didn't have anyone helping us."

"What about these amazing Grandmas that taught you how to cook?"

"They were both gone by the time I was twelve. Thankfully, I spent a lot of time in both their kitchens. I can cook. Brie didn't and lives off cereal, toast, and pop tarts."

"Well, I live off takeout, whatever I steal from Marco, and pancakes."

"Not anymore." I smiled at him.

He pulled me close. "Thankfully, not anymore."

We danced for close to two hours without leaving the dance floor. A non-country slow song came on and I noticed Joey dancing with a beautiful blonde, I'd never seen before. "Who's that?"

"Ally. Joey's ex that he's never gotten over and we all know they'll end up together someday. She just can't do the military life thing. It's too hard to not know if he's safe and where he is. He's not just military. He's special forces. We never know for sure where he is. It was hard on them. Maybe when he's back, they can make it work. Now that's an interesting development." He turned my head to Shauna and Brady on the dance floor.

"Wow, super surprising."

At the end of the song, I realized Marco and Jenna weren't on the dance floor anymore and weren't at the table. Jesse realized what I had noticed. "They left right before the end of the song."

"So, we aren't rude if we leave, because others left first, right?"

"I don't care if it is rude. We leave when you want to leave."

"I want to leave. I do want more dancing though, but not here."

He started laughing and knew instantly what I was talking about. He leaned in close and whispered, "let's go so I can get my Channing Tatum on." We walked out of the bar laughing with my arm around his waist and his arm over my shoulder.

Chapter 13

Jesse

As we pulled into the driveway, I looked over at Lexie.

"Any requests tonight besides a certain dance?"

"I changed my mind. I don't need that dance tonight."

"What would you like, Sweetheart?"

"Strip poker."

"Best Saturday night of my life." I got out of the car and opened her door and took her hand. "So, are you adding any layers to what you are wearing before we start this game?"

She nodded. "NOTHING I have on will be on when I'm done getting ready for this game."

I low growled. "Any rules to how many layers I'm allowed to put on?"

"No more than eight items." I opened the door to the house and let her in. She turned and looked at me. "Go get what you need and take it to the guestroom to get ready, I'll get ready in your room."

"Our room Sweetheart, our room. Works for me. Where do you want to play?"

"On your bed."

"Correction. Our bed."

"Our bed."

We walked into the room and I grabbed clothes from the dresser. "Let me know when you're ready. I'll throw on my clothes and grab the poker stuff."

I took my phone and turned off the ringer and notifications and turned on the sexy playlist that we just made together and put it on the dock before I walked into the bathroom and closed the door to get ready. Once I had layered my eight items, I grabbed my poker stuff and waited and waited and waited. I finally heard "I'm ready."

I walked into the bedroom wearing two sweatshirts and sweatpants with a pair of basketball shorts over them. She lost it and broke down into giggles immediately. "You look ridiculous."

"Eight items. I even counted my socks. You on the other hand look beautiful."

"I think you just layered eight items and I planned mine to get smaller each layer."

I crawled up onto the bed and kissed her. "This is the best idea ever Sweetheart. A great night with friends and now we end the night just the two of us. Thank you."

"You're welcome. Now sit your sexy ass down and let's play." I loved the bossy side she was showing more frequently.

I turned the playlist on and turned the song up just a little. "How's this?"

"Perfect. I love our new playlist."

"Me too." She was shuffling the cards. I asked, "Dealer's choice each hand?"

"Always."

We played our first hand, five-card draw, and she won. I took off one of my sweatshirts using my best sexy stripper moves. She giggled. The next hand was my choice, seven-card stud. I lost my second sweatshirt.

"I thought for sure you'd remove the ridiculous basketball shorts over the sweatpants."

"I thought about it, but it's hot. I'm dying in the sweatshirts."

"Alright, my deal. I choose low ball. The way your calls have fallen tonight, it might be the only way to get me out of one of these layers."

I reached out for her and pulled her closer to me and tickled her sides right in the spot that always sent her into fits of giggles. I kissed her and then let her deal the cards. I lost the ridiculous basketball shorts. I chose Texas hold 'em next, and she finally lost her zip-up sweatshirt. She dealt seven-card stud with deuces wild and I lost my sweatpants. She was in a fit of giggles after watching my attempt at sexy removal of them without getting my lazy butt off the bed.

"That was hilarious." She leaned across and kissed me. She meant it as a soft kiss, but I placed my hand behind her head and pulled her in closer to me deepening the kiss. I slowed us. "Why'd you stop, Jesse?"

"Because you still have seven items and I'm dying to win a few hands so I can watch you take them off. Unless you want to surrender."

"Never. It's your deal."

I dealt Omaha, thinking maybe she might not know that one. She did. I lost a sock. She burst into giggles again. "I feel bad for you and I'm getting hot. I'll give you one for free." She moved from the criss-cross position she was sitting in and moved onto her knees and slowly removed her t-shirt revealing a double layer of tank tops and whatever was under those.

"So sexy Baby. So sexy. Now it's your deal." She chose five-card draw and lost a tank top. The next round was my choice. I chose seven-card stud next and she lost her capris. I had a feeling she'd been letting me win. "You lost at least the last one on purpose."

She shrugged and winked at me. "I'm hot. I needed to remove another layer."

I was down to one sock, my shirt, and my boxer briefs. She had a pair of shorts, a tank top, and whatever she had on under those. I leaned forward and said, "Next round loser takes off everything and then helps the winner take off theirs."

"Deal."

"Nope, it's your deal," I said winking at her. I leaned forward and kissed her. "Deal the cards Sweetheart, either way, it's the last hand."

"Texas hold 'em. Get ready to strip."

"I will gladly strip and then help you out of your shorts and tank, and whatever else is under them."

I lost. I removed my sock first, then my shirt, and then my boxers. Then I moved across the bed to her. I took the deck of cards and set them on the nightstand while leaning across her. Then I kissed her. I moved her toward my side and slid my hands down her side to the hem of her tank. I slowly tugged it up and broke our kiss briefly so I could pull it over her head revealing a light pink lace tank-style bra. "Gorgeous. You are gorgeous." Then I continued my hands down her sides to her waistband and slowly removed her shorts revealing matching lace panties. I grabbed the ties on each side at the same time and pulled the strings. "So gorgeous." I moved my hands back up her side to her bra. I ran my finger across her the edge along her cleavage. She giggled. I traced my fingers down to the bottom edge and then lifted it up and over her head. "Best poker game ever."

"Agreed. I have another present for you."

"Nothing can top this."

She wrapped her arms over my shoulders and positioned herself in my lap. "You pick position. Show me something you like."

I whispered. "I like everything best with you."

"Pick something new. I've loved everything best with you too."

"Okay. I'll pick, but I need to know one thing. Do you still want face to face with lots of eye contact? I have lots of ideas so help me narrow it down."

"Aren't we out of options with that as a possibility?"

"Nowhere close." I leaned forward and kissed her. "Here's what we are going to do, I'm going to sit with my legs straight, and then you sit on top of them with your knees bent over my thighs and take me in as deep as you want. Then we both lean back. If you lean back further, I can work your clit at the same time. Want to try it?"

"Yes!"

"Come here, Baby." I pulled her over to me and had her straddle across me. I moved my right hand up her inner thigh and began working slow circles on her clit. I increased the intensity of the circles and then moved a finger inside her. I moved in and out slowly and continued to work circles on her clit slowly. "Faster, you're teasing me."

"But it's fun to tease you." I laughed. She playfully smacked my shoulder. I increased the speed of the circles and just before she was there. I positioned her over me. "Are you ready?" She nodded. I removed my fingers and guided her down to take me in and then gave her control. She leaned back. "You good Baby?"

"So good! Faster." I increased our speed and she reached for my hand to guide me back to her clit. "Please." I worked in slow circles. "Stop teasing me. Faster!" I gave her what she wanted and thrust into her faster and harder, she came hard screaming out my name before collapsing. "That was amazing."

"So amazing." I pulled her onto my chest and repositioned us into a more comfortable position to sleep. "Sleep Sweetheart. Sleep." I grabbed the edged of the comforter and threw it over us. Wrapping us cocoon style.

"I love you, Jesse."

"I love you, Lexie."

We slept until her alarm went off four hours later. "Weekend. Why is your alarm on? It's Sunday."

"I promised Jenna we'd be there by nine to help with breakfast. I didn't expect to be up until almost four, but it was so worth it. Last night, well this morning, was so amazing. Thank you, Jesse."

"I love you, Sweetheart. I'm going to give you everything and I'm going to make all the bad memories disappear."

"They already are Jesse. I know it's barely been a month, but I feel like a whole new person." She rolled to face me, and I took her lips and gently kissed her. After kissing for almost an hour, she slowed us and pulled away. "Ugh, we need to get going."

"Okay, but more kissing later. Lots more kissing." I kissed her one more time before we got ready and headed to the house to spend the day with everyone.

We got to the house just as Marco was returning from picking up Gabby. We met them in the yard outside. "Hey Gabby, did you have fun at your mom's?" I eyed Marco trying to figure out why Gabby was home early.

"We made bracelets yesterday, then this morning she asked me to call Daddy to see if I could come home early because she got invited to something. Daddy said he can always get me early. We're going to make breakfast and then plan something fun." She turned and looked at Lexie. "Hi, Ms. Lexie. Are you Jesse's girlfriend now?"

"I am. Can I come in and help you make breakfast? I promised Jenna I'd help with food today."

"Sure. Do you know what we're having? I hope it's pancakes or waffles. Or maybe the waffles Jenna makes me for special treats with chocolate and marshmallows."

"No clue. Let's go ask Jenna."

Lexie went into the house with Gabby and I turned to Marco. "You're joking? Again? Does she ever finish visitation days?"

"No. She hasn't for almost a year. I always get a call to come to get her early. I'm used to it. I know the day will come when she just stops visits altogether. It's heartbreaking. Thankfully, Gabby has all of you."

Marco and I found Lexie, Gabby, and Jenna in the kitchen working on breakfast until Joey came in and stole his Gabby monster and let her start the *My Little Pony* movie. Better him, than me because I was totally over that movie after time one hundred and sixty-seven. Lexie laughed when I told her that all of us had kept track of how many times we watched it. Jenna was at three hundred and eighty-four the last time we reported numbers proving to everyone that she was the true rock star of the group. Lexie and Jenna made pancakes and waffles for everyone and then we all chose activities for the day. Jenna and Marco went on their first real date. Shauna and Brady headed to the movies.

Lexie and I went to the indoor jump place and for ice cream with Joey and Gabby. Joey had promised Gabby at least one fun thing each day he was home. He takes his role as Godfather seriously and makes sure he spends as much time with her as possible when he's home. "Wow, this place is huge." Lexie's eyes were adorably cute and wide when she walked in.

"You've never been here?" I wrapped my arm around her waist.

"No. It's a kid jump place. Why would I have been here?"

I shook my head. "It's not just for kids. They have a full kid's zone and kids ninja zone and activities, but they also have all of that for adults as well as the trampoline areas. There's even a glow-in-the-dark room."

"Is that why you told me to wear the yellow and pink?"

"Yes. It will show up better under the black lights. We also have glow bracelets and necklaces. Gabby and I are pros at this. You're going to love it." I paid for Lexie and I and tried to pay for Joey and Gabby, but I was too late, he had already tried to pay for us, so we called it even by each paying for our own dates.

Joey headed to the kid's area with Gabby and I took Lexie to the adult zone and we decided to meet in the glow room in an hour. I bet her five kisses that I could make it through the ninja zone faster than her and lost.

"I'll take my kisses like this: one on each cheek, each side of my neck, and right here" as she pointed to her lips. I gently kissed each cheek, then each side of her neck, and then her lips.

"I love losing bets to you Sweetheart because I end up with the best prizes anyway." I led her to the glow room. Joey and Gabby were waiting for us. I took bracelets and necklaces out of my cargo short pockets and passed them between the four of us. We bounced in the glow room for almost two hours before Gabby said she was going to pass out and only ice cream could cure her. Then we headed next door for ice cream.

Joey told Gabby she could get whatever she wanted. Her eyes got wide. I pulled the responsible uncle card. "He means any flavor. You know you're only allowed a kid scoop. The scoops are huge."

Joey shook his head. "I meant to get whatever you want. What do you want Princess?"

"Double scoop strawberry cheesecake and chocolate raspberry swirl."

Joey ordered the double scoop with two spoons. "We'll share. Those are my favorite too."

Gabby looked at us. "This is our double date. You should get a double scoop and share too. Then we can be twin dates."

Lexie laughed. "That sounds like a great idea." She looked at me. "Let's each pick one flavor and share."

"Sounds like a great idea. You pick first."

"Caramel chocolate brownie crunch."

"My favorite. I'm excited. My second favorite is chocolate peppermint." Lexie giggled. "What's funny Sweetheart?"

"That's my second favorite too."

"I'm not surprised at all by the fact we like the same ice cream flavors. Just more proof, this was meant to be." I pulled her in close to me and kissed her quickly.

"Gross. You two are gross. You're as bad a Joey and Ally used to be and how Daddy and Jenna have been. So gross. Kissing is so gross. I'm never kissing. It's disgusting." Gabby was so loud even from across the room and Joey was cracking up. "Stop kissing all the time."

Lexie turned bright red. "We don't kiss all the time Gabby. We kiss just the right amount of time. Some day you will like kissing, but not until you're at least twenty."

"Thirty." Joey and I said at the same time.

Gabby laughed. "Daddy said forty and Jenna said fifteen." Joey and I looked at each other and laughed. We both knew that Jenna said fifteen because that's the first time she kissed Marco and she had compared everything to him ever since. We finished our double scoops and then Joey asked Gabby what she wanted to do next. "Arcade. Please. Can we go?"

Joey looked at us. "Are you okay with it?"

"Yeah, that works for me," I said, and I looked at Lexie. "I'll win you a teddy bear." I pulled her close to my side while we walked out of the ice cream shop and Joey threw Gabby onto his shoulders. The arcade was at the end of the same shopping center as the bounce place and ice cream shop, so we walked.

As soon as we were inside, Gabby looked at Joey and me. "You should compete for who can win their date the best prize. Best will be judged by the biggest." We agreed. What we didn't tell her is once I had enough tickets for the small teddy bear I wanted to get Lexie, we were combining tickets to make sure she got the giant pink bunny rabbit she has had her eye on for months.

When we headed back to the house, Gabby informed us that "just because abuela's not home doesn't mean you can wear scrubby clothes to Sunday dinner." After Lexie helped Jenna with the bulk of dinner prep, we headed back to the house to put on fancy clothes. I put on the outfit I wore for our at-home fancy dinner and Lexie chose an off-shoulder black dress that hit mid-thigh.

I came up behind her at the bathroom counter while she finished her makeup. I placed one hand on each side of the counter and pressed into her. I kissed her neck. "You are gorgeous. Are you sure we need to go back to dinner? Can we stay at home?"

"We promised Gabby we'd be at dinner. Let's go enjoy friends and then come home."

When we got back to the house Gabby was playing board games with Ally and Joey. Brady and Shauna were sitting at the picnic table in the backyard playing dominoes and Jenna and Marco were on the back steps talking. "Hey Ally, it's great to see you. This is Lexie."

"Hi, Ally. It's nice to meet you."

"You too," Ally replied from where she was sitting with Gabby.

Lexie looked at me. "I'm going to go check on the food. Some stuff should be ready. Jesse, can you help me? Let's give Jenna a break tonight."

I looked over to Joey. "Joey, can you help me extend the table? Then Gabby and I can set it." He stood up and quickly kissed Ally.

Gabby picked up his piece off the board and dropped it into the box. "You automatically lose when you leave the game."

He called back, "I know."

Lexie took over the rest of the dinner prep and then called everyone in for dinner. Gabby prayed while we were standing around the table before sitting and then we ate, and we ate, and we ate. If you left this table hungry it was your fault. There was a tray of rice and beans on each end, next to a salad bowl, then a tray of enchiladas and a platter of flautas. The chili verde sat in the center of the table. Four tortilla warmers packed full of tortillas were placed around the table along with sour cream, guacamole, and two types of salsa.

"Damn. You all made way too much food. I forgot how good Sunday dinners are in this house. I cannot wait until I'm here every week again." Joey stood from the table and started clearing plates.

Once dishes were washed and leftovers were packed away and Gabby was in bed, Shauna and Brady set up dominoes and were joined by Ally and Joey. Marco and Jenna headed to bed. Lexie and I decided to head home. "I have to work tomorrow, and we will be busy since Marco's off half the day.

Lexie works in the morning and then will be here to hang with Gabby while Jenna and Marco are at her appointment."

When we were home, Lexie asked me shyly, "we aren't sleeping yet, are we?"

"No Sweetheart, we're not. Not unless you want to. What do you want?"

"Slow and sweet and then fall asleep kissing."

"That sounds like the best way to fall asleep." I gave her slow and sweet twice before kissing until we fell asleep. When my alarm went off for work in the morning, she got up and made me breakfast and packed my coffee and lunch.

"I'll be at Marco's to watch Gabby until they're back from the appointment or until Joey gets there. He said he can watch her the rest of the day once he's back at the house. We can either eat there or I can make dinner here."

"Here. Today will be a hard day for Jenna, so let's plan on being here. You'll be busy with Gabby, so I can pick up takeout."

"I'll do something easy. We have everything for an easy veggie pasta dish. I can have dinner ready in about 20 minutes."

"That sounds amazing. Thank you for breakfast and for packing my lunch. I'll see you tonight." I pulled her into me and kissed her deeply before slowing us and heading to work.

The rest of our week flew by. Wednesday night, Mom was home from her trip, and we had family dinner. Jenna had decided she was ready to come home for good and she and Marco had spent their day off getting her stuff from her apartment in the city. This one-week test drive they had been on was just what they needed to realize no relationship before had worked because they were in a relationship with the wrong person. Gabby announced that she asked for a puppy and was told no, so she was going to ask for a baby brother every day until she got one. Joey officially announced that he'd be home for good in three months and he'd be moving in with Ally when he got back. I decided since we were making announcements that I'd let everyone know that I had convinced Lexie to stay forever and she was moving in. Mom gave me "the look" when I said forever.

After dinner, she took me to her house on the back of the property and gave me a small box. "This was your great-grandma's. It's now yours to give to Lexie when you're ready."

"What about Marco?"

"He has one, the one his dad gave me that belong to your great-great-grandma. Tony will get another family ring when it's time. I was in charge of choosing who got each ring and I think I've picked perfectly."

I opened the box and knew it was perfect. "It's perfect." It was a dainty band with two diamonds on each side and a larger stone set inside a heart.

"I heard you call her Sweetheart and I'm so glad I chose this ring for you."

"It's perfect. It's absolutely perfect. I took her to the hot springs out on my mom's family's property. She met Aunt Maria."

"I heard. Maria called me. She told me to get the ring ready."

"Well, I'm not giving it to her tonight."

"You'll know when it's time. Now you have it for when you're ready."

"Thanks, Mom."

We walked back to the house and as soon as I saw her, I knew I was ready. I was ready to commit to long-term and hearing Gabby talk about baby brothers at dinner made me realize I liked the idea of kids. I think it was time for us to have one of our talks.

Chapter 14

Lexie

I was prepping salad and veggies in Marco's kitchen with Mom and Jenna. I had come over to help with Friday night family dinner after teaching studio classes. Gabby was in my last class, so I just brought her home with me and saved Jenna a trip back. "I can't believe that Joey's trip is almost over, and this is our last night."

"I know. It's gone so fast and so many things have changed. We still need to get the dirty details from Shauna about her movie dates with Brady because I'm pretty sure that movie is a code word for something else." Mom laughed. I laughed. Jenna laughed after she said it.

About ten minutes later Jenna and I both said "the guys are home" at the same time. We looked at each other and laughed. Mom laughed and less than a minute later Marco and Jesse walked in the door.

Mom said, "it looks like Lexie has the same skill Jenna has and knows exactly when Jesse arrives somewhere."

Jesse looked at me as he walked across the living room to the kitchen. "I like that." He pulled me into a hug and I quickly kissed him. "I need a shower, but I wanted to say hi and tell you I missed you today. I'm going to go shower quickly and I'll be out to help with the rest of the dinner stuff. Marco and Jenna are going on a sunset ride, so I'll help get dinner stuff done and Joey and Ally are going to entertain Gabby."

"Sounds good. When you're ready, I'll go change into my dress. Then I'm all set."

After dinner, we all gathered in the living room for one last family night. Gabby insisted she could make it through the movie and was asleep ten minutes in. We had our usual spot on the L-shaped couch and Joey and Ally had the other spot. No one could choose a movie so all four of us girls yelled out "*A Walk to Remember,*" sending everyone into fits of laughter. Joey said "what the hell. It's a tradition. Let's find out what Jenna thinks of it this time." All of us fell asleep and Jenna never did give her opinion of the movie this time.

Joey's alarm went off way too early for any of us at four. He and Brady needed to be at the airport in a couple of hours. The plan had been to say goodbye last night but everyone fell asleep in the living room, so we were all up and were able to say goodbye. He spent time with mom in her little house before waking Gabby to say goodbye and tucking her back into bed. He sat with Jenna on the back steps and the rest of us said goodbye in the front yard.

When he got to me, he pulled me into a hug and said, "I think you might be the best thing that's ever happened to him."

I hugged him and whispered, "He's the best thing that's ever happened to me."

Jesse stood behind me and wrapped me in his arms as Joey continued his goodbyes. "He's right. You're the best thing that's happened to me. I have the day off. You have the day off. Go somewhere with me?"

"Anywhere."

He asked Jenna if I could borrow her helmet and gear again and we headed home to get the bike. We rode about thirty minutes outside of town. He pulled the bike onto a dirt road and opened a private gate. We rode through and he stopped to close the gate. He took us up the path to a hill. When we stopped, I took my helmet off. "Where are we?"

"A friend's property. It has the best view of Woods Lake. It's where most of us came to learn to drive and race."

"I know how to drive, why I am here?"

"Because other than my family's property, this is my favorite place and it's filled with so many memories, I wanted to share it with you."

"I love it. Thank you for bringing me."

I was still sitting behind him. He guided me off the bike and then back on this time sitting in front of him facing him. "You're welcome. Do you want to learn to drive the bike?"

"Yes." He gave me all the safety information and then he positioned us on the bike so he could help me. It was the most incredible experience and something I never knew I would want to do. Jesse was the absolute best boyfriend because he pushed me to try new things by making those things safe.

We spent the rest of the day on the property practicing my driving skills. We ordered take out and picked it up on our way home and ate it out of the containers while watching *NCIS*. When the timer went off on the oven, Jesse leaped off the couch and was excited to find layered brownies ready. He set the pan on a trivet on the coffee table. He topped the brownies with ice cream and brought over two spoons. We finished about half the pan of brownies before falling asleep on the couch. Around two, he carried me to our bed.

The next morning, he woke me at eight. "Want to go to the hot springs?" I jumped up and started getting ready. We rode out to the property, stopping to get the key and lunch from Maria. This time we walked to the hot spring that was the furthest from the picnic table on the same path as the first one.

"Tell me about this one. The last one was your favorite because it was for two and middle temperate."

"This one is still big enough for two and only slightly warmer. This one has my favorite view." I took off my shorts and tank top revealing my super skimpy bikini. He helped me into the springs. "It's a little deeper than the other." He guided me to sit with him.

"Remember when we had our talk on my couch about moving from friendship to more?"

"Of course, I remember that conversation. I remember everything, Jesse."

He wrapped his arms around me tighter and pulled me to him. "I told you when one of us needed something to change, we'd just talk about it."

"Okay," I said slowly almost like I was worried about something.

He rested his chin on my shoulder. "I need to ask you something. When we started hanging out, we were friends with no intention of a relationship. Then we decided to start this and just see what happens. I told you from the start, I had no desire to do the marriage and kid thing."

"Right. I was okay with that because I wasn't in this for a relationship."

"Now that it's a relationship, what are your thoughts on marriage and kids?"

"They haven't changed. I still want that someday."

"Good. Because I want that too. I've never seen myself as someone who should get married and have kids because I didn't have an example of how to be a husband or father, but I realize that every relationship is different. We can make things work the way we need them to. I always say I'm an open book, so I'm just going to ask. Do you think you'd want to have kids with me someday?"

I turned and looked over my shoulder at him. I looked deep into his dark brown eyes and made sure my eyes were locked on his as I spoke. "I don't think so. I know so. I want to be a mom, specifically, I want to be a mom to your kids. I want lots of babies Jesse. Like you might need to add a room or two on to the house for them."

"I like that idea Sweetheart." He leaned forward and gently took my lips with his kissing me sweetly.

"Any specific reason we are having this conversation?"

"I just needed to be sure that we were on the same page."

"Okay."

"I love you, Lexie." He rotated me so I was facing him and positioned me so I was straddled across his lap. "I know this is fast and we are having this conversation way sooner than I would expect, but I just needed to know we were on the same page."

I leaned forward and kissed him. "We are. We are definitely on the same page."

"I love you. From the first night we hung out in the bar, I knew there was something different about you. You're smart, funny, kind, talented, gorgeous, and can cook both food food and baked food. You make me laugh. You make me smile. I love coming home to find you in the kitchen, sketching on the studio porch, or reading on the couch. I love quiet nights at home with you more than anything. I love that you trust me to keep you safe enough to try new things. I love it when you're bossy and that you tell me what you want. You have completely changed my life for the better just by being in it. I love you, Lexie. I know I asked you to stay for the week so I could make sure you were safe and then I asked you to stay forever. I mean forever forever. I want you to fill my house with your things and your art and make it a home. As soon as you decide you are ready, I will give you as many babies as you want." He reached for the small box he had hidden in the rocks next to us and opened it. "I want you to not just move in as my girlfriend, but as my wife. Will you marry me?"

"Jesse, this is the best day of my life. Yes! I know it's fast, but I don't want to wait. I've known since a week after I was invited to see your house that I wanted to stay forever. Yes. I'll marry you." He slid the ring on her finger, and it fit perfectly. I looked at it. "It's perfect. It's a heart because I'm your Sweetheart. I love it."

"It was my great-grandma's. Mom has a family ring for me, Marco, and Tony. This one is perfect for you. I love you."

I leaned forward and kissed him. "I love you too Jesse. Can I ask you a question?"

"Anything."

"How soon do you want to get married?"

"Today. Tomorrow. A month from now. Six months from now. A year from now. Whatever you want."

"Let's do it as soon as Joey's home. That way our whole family is together. When do you want to start having babies?"

"As soon as you do."

"Now. No more birth control."
"Deal."

Chapter 15

Jesse

The next month flew by. Marco and Tony helped me move Lexie's stuff into the house. We sold the stuff she didn't need anymore. I had become completely spoiled coming home to her in the studio sketching every night or in the kitchen. This morning I was surprising her with breakfast with friends before the end of summer festival art exhibit.

"Good morning, Sweetheart." I pulled her in close to me and kissed along her neck as we woke up.

She scooted back against me and turned her head to look over her shoulder. "Good morning."

"Go ahead and take a shower and get dressed. I have a surprise for you before the festival."

When we were both ready, I led her out to the car. When I pulled into Rocky's parking lot, she looked at me. "What are we doing here on a Saturday morning?"

"It's walking distance to the festival, so we don't have to battle street parking and I needed to stop by and help Rocky with something first." I got out of the car and walked around to her side to get her door. I led her inside and she saw all of our family: Marco, Jenna, Gabby, Mom, Rocky, Tony, Shauna, and Ally, and a table covered in food.

"What is all of this? Why is everyone here?" Lexie looked at me and then around at everyone in the room.

"Family brunch before your art show. I know all the kids are showing pieces, but you have an entire booth and are practically your own show. We wanted to celebrate you. Mom, Jenna, and Ally made most of the food. Rocky is providing the mimosa bar, and Shauna ordered those amazing pecan cinnamon rolls that you love from the fancy bakery." I pulled her into my side and wrapped my arm around her. "I'm so proud of you and how hard you've worked, and we all wanted to celebrate you this morning and then go to the festival as a family."

Her eyes filled with tears and she spoke quietly, the way she does when she's feeling emotional. "You guys, this is so amazing. Thank you. I didn't even expect any of you to come to the festival, so I wasn't expecting this. Thank you."

Marco spoke first. "Family is always the most important thing to all of us Lexie. You're family. We can't wait to see the artwork and Gabby let us know that each student chose one piece for the auction to help fund the art program. I'm prepared to outbid anyone to bring home Gabby's piece and Tony and Rocky are going to bid on any pieces that don't have a bid, so all the kids' pieces are bought."

Rocky spoke up. "That wall behind you has always been covered in local sports memorabilia and it's a huge wall. I'll rearrange it and put artwork up too. It's time we valued more than just sports around here. Let's eat breakfast and head to the festival."

Everyone filled their plates and made fancy mimosas or mocktails at their bar before grabbing a spot at one of the tables and enjoying time together as a family. After a huge breakfast, we all walked to the square where the community center was and found the student pieces. By the time Marco got there to bid, Gabby's piece had three other bids, so he jumped the bid by one hundred dollars hoping to snag it. He set his phone to alert 15 minutes before the auction ended so he could be back in time to check on the status of his bid before the auction closed. He ended up having to add another fifty dollars to the bid to bring it home.

Everything in Lexie's booth was for sale but the sketch she'd worked on daily for the first month we'd been together was an auction item. When I saw it, I smiled. "It's me." I turned at looked at her.

She nodded. "It is. It started just you and then I decided to add the garage at the house and bike with all your tools. It was such a fun piece to work on. I never expected there to be so much interest, but it looks like there's already a couple of bids."

I outbid the current high bid by two hundred dollars. "I'm taking this home."

"You're ridiculous. I can always do another one." She slid her arm around my waist, and I put my arm over her shoulders.

"I want this one because it's what you worked on for the first month that we were together. I love it." I pulled her in close and kissed her.

"I love you, Jesse."

"I love you, Lexie. Let's go check on the other pieces and see what's selling so far."

By the end of the festival, every art piece had been sold from the student pieces. All of Lexie's pieces sold, including two that I bought for the house and three that Rocky bought for the bar. I got the drawing. My bid jump had worked. In the end, Lexie's art show idea had worked. The community center raised almost four thousand dollars to fund additional art programs which meant Lexie could teach in town three days a week and two days a week in the city for the two sessions. Over time as the art program grew, she was hoping to teach full time in town and add classes for teens and adults.

The next two months passed by quickly. We planned a small backyard wedding in the middle of November, two weeks after Joey was home for good.

"Take a deep breath. You can do this." Jenna was right, Marco's voice is always calming. We were standing in the side yard facing the backyard. The yard was filled with chairs for our family and friends.

"I never would have thought I would be doing this at all, but definitely not the first one of us to do this." I looked between Marco and Joey as I said it.

"Neither did we man. Mine's in a couple of months though, so you're not too far ahead of us. I always figured Joey would be first." Marco put his hand on my shoulder.

"Maybe if we hadn't had a break. I've only been home for two weeks. Give me time to enjoy sleeping in the same bed with her every night again. I've got a ring and I have a plan, but I need a couple of months."

Music started to play, and we walked from where we were in the side yard to the crab apple tree in the back corner of the backyard. Marco was by my side and Joey was next to him. Tony wasn't standing with me because he offered to walk Lexie down the aisle to me since she didn't have anyone in her family to do it and he'd thought of her as a little sister since she was three and he was five.

The music changed and the studio porch door opened. Gabby walked out first. She hugged me and then Marco and Joey before sitting with Mom and Rocky. Then Brie walked down followed by Jenna. I heard Marco gasp when he saw Jenna. They were each wearing lavender knee-length dresses. Brie's was strapless and Jenna's had a halter-style neckline. They were carrying purple irises from our flower garden tied with a white ribbon. I had cut the flowers that morning and Gabby had chosen her bouquet about an hour before everyone started to arrive. She chose one of every color from our yard and then asked me to tie a pink and white ribbon around them for her.

The music changed one more time and Lexie appeared. Tony met her at the bottom step to walk her down to me. She looked beautiful in her knee-length sweetheart cut white dress. She was carrying a bouquet of white and pink roses and purple irises from our garden. Tony gave her a hugged and then placed her hands in mine before taking his seat next to Gabby. We exchanged traditional vows and made promises to always make each other laugh, eat dessert straight from the pan, and be open books. I leaned in and whispered a promise to always follow the "ladies first" rule which sent her into a fit of giggles. Our backyard wedding with barbecue reception was perfect for us and the chocolate dessert buffet was better than any wedding cake could have been.

That night after everyone had left, I climbed into bed with my beautiful wife and pulled her close to me. "Today was perfect. I couldn't have asked for a better wedding and wouldn't have changed a thing."

"It was perfect Jesse."

"Now that your stuff is completely moved in, do you have any requests?"

"Furniture." She turned in my arms to face me.

"What room? I'll buy you anything you want for any room in the house."

She smiled and kissed me sweetly. "The nursery. You have 32 weeks to get that guestroom redecorated."

I got the biggest smile on my face and pulled her in close. "You tell me what you want in there and I'll get it."

Epilogue

~ ~ ~ ~

Jesse

~ ~ ~ ~

Elizabeth "Ellie" Ann Sanchez was born exactly on her due date in July. We named her after Jenna and Mom giving her both of their middle names as her name. She was the spitting image of her mama with light brown hair that looked auburn in the sun and blue eyes that sometimes looked gray. She stole my heart as quickly as her Mama had a little over a year ago.

She became a big sister sixteen months later when Gabrielle "Gabe" Jesus Sanchez was born. I kept the tradition of Jesus as the middle name for the boys in my family and gave him Rocky's legal name. Over the years Rocky had been more a father to me than my own.

Nineteen months after Gabe, Antonia "Toni" Brianne, named after Tony and Brie, joined our family. When Lexie said she wanted lots of babies starting immediately, she meant it. Three kids in three-and-a-half years were a lot, but she wasn't done fulfilling dreams. In addition to being home with the three kids all day, she continued to teach studio classes at the community center in Woods Lake two days a week and we had recently started renovating an old building to turn it into the art center she had always dreamed of.

~ ~ ~ ~

Lexie

~ ~ ~ ~

In the five years we've been married, Jesse has made all of my dreams come true. We just opened the art center that I've always dreamed of. We have three beautiful children and he just finished the remodel on the house to build us a master suite so the kids could finally spread out and not be in one room anymore.

Thanks to Ally and Joey braving a house filled with kids, we had a quiet evening at home planned. I put on eight items and somehow managed to make my top layer the dress I wore for our first at home fancy date night. It was tighter in the hips and thighs after three babies and it showed my tummy a bit, but I knew Jesse wouldn't care.

"Sweetheart, you look gorgeous. I do not know how you have on eight items right now, but I cannot wait to see what they are." Jesse pulled me close to him and kissed me deeply. When he pulled away, he said, "I smell chocolate." I moved to the side and showed him the three desserts I had made.

"I couldn't decide so I made double fudge rocky road brownies like from our first apartment hangout. I made chocolate lasagna because it's become your favorite. Last but not least, chocolate cheesecake with raspberry sauce."

"My three favorite memories. We're having a chocolate dessert buffet for dinner?"

"And pizza. I ordered pepperoni pizza like from our first day together."

"Best at-home date ever."

"You say that every date."

"Because they just keep getting better Sweetheart." He pulled me in close and kissed me. When he pulled away, he handed me a plate. "Ladies first."

I grabbed a slice of each dessert and two pieces of pizza. He did the same but cut bigger slices and four pieces of pizzas. We sat at the table and talked for hours. As he cleaned dishes and put leftovers away, I grabbed the poker stuff and the gift. He came into the bedroom and set his phone on the dock turning on our latest playlist.

"What's this?" He asked as he held up the present.

"A present."

"Not what I meant."

"It's a because I love you present."

He smiled before unwrapping it. He looked at the framed photo and then looked at me. "Seriously?"

"Yes."

"I'm so excited!"

"I was so scared you'd freak out. We had three in three-and-a-half years, so I thought maybe after the eighteen-month break, you'd want to be done."

"As many babies as you want, remember?" He pulled me close and asked, "how far along?"

"Fifteen weeks."

"I surrender in poker. I will gladly strip before helping you out of your clothes and celebrate."

I laughed and said "Pony!" He cracked up and found the song on the playlist and proceeded to give me the most hilarious striptease.

Emilia Alexis was born two weeks early and completed our family. In a family full of Emilios, no one had ever named one of the girls Emilia. I thought my husband was a genius for thinking of it and when he suggested Alexis as the middle name my eyes filled with tears. "She's the perfect combination of us and now our names. All the other kids are so strongly you or me. She's the perfect baby to complete our family." Jesse had his arms wrapped around both of us lounging on our bed while the other three kids were at Marco and Jenna's for a movie afternoon. "Why did you look sad when I said the last baby?" I asked quietly while looking deep into his eyes.

"In five and a half years of marriage and six years of being with you, you have given me more than I could have ever imagined wanting. It's just a little sad to know that we are coming to an end of our firsts. Feeling first kicks; first night home; all those things are ending, but a whole new series of firsts are beginning. I'm not sad, I'm just reflecting." He repositioned so he was leaning on the pillows against the headboard and he book Emilia from me and placed her on his chest, so her head was resting between his shoulder and neck. He placed his right hand on her back holding in place and used his left arm to guide me up onto his shoulder. I snuggled in close, laying on my right side, and placed my left arm across his stomach. He pulled the cover over me and placed his left hand on my hip. This was our favorite way to sleep with babies in bed with us. He held the baby and me in his arms and every part of me was touching him which was always my favorite way to sleep.

After we were repositioned, I spoke softly. "I love everything we've built together too, Jesse. I love our life and I wouldn't change anything. I'm so excited about all the new firsts, but I get it. It's hard to realize that we are saying goodbye to some of the firsts." I reached over to my nightstand and picked up a manilla envelope. "I have a present for you." I handed him the envelope. He opened it and pulled out the sketch I had done of him sitting in his recliner holding Emilia surrounded by the rest of the kids.

"Sweetheart, I love it. I'm hanging it on the wall right next to the sketch you did of me the first month you spent in the house as soon as I get a frame for it. Thank you."

"I still can't believe you outbid by two hundred dollars to get that sketch at the end of summer festival." I smiled and slightly laughed when I said it.

"I wanted it. I loved it then and I still love it. I love that we've filled this home with all your work." He pulled me close and kissed me. "We've made a great life together Lexie. Thank you for being my only mean something."

"Thank you for loving me so much so that I was able to forget all the bad memories. Thank you for helping me make all my dreams come true and for being my only mean something. I love you, Jesse."

"I love you, Lexie."

NOTES

If you liked this book, please let me know!

Website:
https://www.authorjlynnautumn.com

Facebook Page:
http://www.facebook.com/AuthorJLynnAutumn

Facebook Fan Chat Group:
http://www.facebook.com/groups/JabberingWithJLynn

Instagram:
http://www.instagram.com/AuthorJLynnAutumn

Goodreads:
http://www.goodreads.com/AuthorJLynnAutumn

You can also help spread the word by recommending the book to your friends or by buying them a digital copy that can be sent right to the Kindle App on any device.

You can also help spread the word by reviewing the book on Amazon and Goodreads and sharing the posts about the book from my Facebook page.

Thank you!

Additional Books by JLynn Autumn

<u>Game Changer Series</u>

Game Changer (Game Changer Book 1)

Life Changer (Game Changer Book 2 – Mark & Linda) *Coming 2021*

Life List (Game Change Book 3 – Holly & Greg) *Coming 2021*

<u>Woods Lake Series</u>
"It's Always Been You" (Woods Lake Book 1)

"You Mean Something" (Woods Lake Book 2)

"A Woods Lake Christmas" (Woods Lake Book 3 - Christmas novella) December 2020

<u>Woods Lake Series Coming in 2021 – Currently Untitled</u>

"I Never Stopped Loving You" (Woods Lake Book 4) - January 2021.

Additional stories for Shauna, Tony, Brie, and Matt will be published in 2021.

About the Author

JLynn Autumn is a part-time writer who dreams of the day she can be a full-time writer. She's a lifelong bookworm. She's a reader, a writer, and an advocate. She's passionate about social justice, education reform, and special education service equity. She is married to her "game changer." The man who showed her that being made a priority and treated with respect should be the standard not the exception. They have one daughter, who is sassy, bossy, opinionated, and keeps them on their toes. JLynn Autumn thinks coffee is a magic liquid that brings her to life most mornings; pizza and tacos should be their own food group; late nights are always better than early mornings; houseplants are a waste of space and will always be forgotten about and die; and that poodles and poodle mixes are the best pets. She's a huge fan of snark, sarcasm, and happily ever after in real life and in books.

Playlist

Hey Jealousy, Gin Blossoms
Can't Sleep, Blacktop Mojo
Ophelia, The Lumineers
Southern Delta – US, Jonathan Elias
I Wanna Be Down, Brandy
In Your Eyes, Lena Hall
Nice & Slow, Usher
Until I Met You, The Sunstreak
Hail the Queen, HYLLS
Better Than Gold, Kevin Daniel
Hey Rachel, Jesse Labelle
Pony, Ginuwine
Wild Love, James Bay
Unsteady, X Ambassadors
Hunting Season, Nikki's Wives
Here with Me, Ready Steady Steroids
Big, Big Plans, Chris Lane

Made in the USA
Las Vegas, NV
03 January 2021